SMOKE ON THE WATER

WAYWARD SONS
BOOK 0

HARPER JACKSON

TAKE THE LEAP PUBLISHING

1

HOYT

"You're going to regret this."

I ignored the warning in my brother Drew's voice and grinned at the keys I now held to the two-story shingle-style house that was all mine. Or would be in another thirty years, when I finished making all the payments to the bank. "It's going to be great."

"I can't believe you bought it without doing more than a video tour."

"There's not that much on the market in my price range. If I wanted to close as soon as I got back on-island, I had to move quickly or risk being forced to move back in with Mom and Dad while I looked." While I loved my parents, after five years away, the last thing I needed was my well-intentioned mom smothering me now that I was home. So I'd come straight from the ferry to the lawyer's office to sign the closing paperwork.

"If you think buying *that* house is gonna keep Mom out of your business, you're sorely mistaken. It's a shithole, Hoyt."

"I concede it looks kinda rough." Something I'd willfully overlooked when the realtor had sent me pictures while I was still in Raleigh. "But it's got good bones. That kind of golden-age construction is worth preserving."

"It's a duplex. Are you planning on adding landlord as a secondary occupation?"

"No. I'm gonna turn it back into a single-family home." It was why I'd come back to Sutter's Ferry and Hatterwick. To sink some roots and start a family. Even though I hadn't actually found the woman yet. I figured by the time I was done working on the house, she'd have turned up, and I'd be ready. "I don't mind living in a construction zone, and with my 24-on, 48-off schedule, I ought to be able to do a solid amount of work on it. No way would I have been able to get that much square footage that close to the ocean without going for a fixer-upper. I was lucky to get this one, as is. The other interested party wanted to tear it down and build something else." Probably more of the mega-mansions that were popping up like mushrooms around the island as Mother Nature cleared the way and locals lost out to mainland investors who had more capital to sink into such a project.

"I'm not sure whoever that was had the wrong idea. But if it makes you happy, who am I to judge?" Drew clapped me on the shoulder. "C'-mon. Let's get a celebratory drink. With that albatross, I suspect you're gonna need one."

"You buying?"

He heaved a put-upon sigh, but I didn't miss the twinkle in his blue eyes. "I mean, since you just sank everything you have into a house, I guess I am."

I swung an arm around shoulders that I'd swear had doubled in width since I left the island five years ago. "Good of you, little bro."

We piled into my truck to make the drive across town from the lawyer's office to the tavern. Nothing on Hatterwick was far, as the entire island was only thirteen miles long and less than three miles at its widest point. The only actual town was the village of Sutter's Ferry, so named for the one way on or off the island. That ferry had been running for more than a hundred and fifty years, though it was no longer a Sutter at the helm, which many said was a damned shame. The heiress of that founding family had married some stuffed-shirt muckity-muck the third, who believed he was above the hard work of manual labor. But the senior Sutters still lived in the big house at the north end of the island. So far as I knew, they were still doing their best to support the island economy, such as it was. That had meant adding additional ferry service to nearby Ocracoke to bring in the tourists more easily. Apparently it had worked, because those tourist dollars had allowed the fire department to expand enough to hire me.

I'd been back to Hatterwick a couple times a year for family holidays, but those trips had been fast and focused on home. This was the first time I'd actually paid attention to the changes in the village. On the way through town proper, I spotted a sign at Hook, Line and Sinker, the fishing supply shop, announcing jet skis and paddleboat rentals. Beyond that, a shiny new sign announced the Pelican Point Beach Bistro and Bar, which had still been a construction site when I'd been back at Christmas. There was no sign anywhere of the unresolved tragedy that had shaken the bedrock of the community two years before. Pedestrian traffic filled the sidewalks, moving in and out of assorted boutique gift shops, and there were definitely more vehicles congesting the roads than those of the locals. But it wasn't until I wheeled into the parking lot of the Tidewater Tavern and spotted a sign announcing OBX Brew House that I finally voiced the general "What the fuck?" that had been simmering in the back of my brain.

"Don't worry. Ed still owns the place. But Bree convinced him to rename it and do a little spiffing up to appeal to the tourist crowd."

Bree Cartwright had been the talk of the village gossip network when she'd been left with her grandfather as a skinny little eight-year-old. If anybody knew what became of her parents, it wasn't common knowledge. She was Ed's, so she belonged to Hatterwick. I vaguely recalled she'd been in Drew's class, or maybe the one below. I guess that made her old enough to be working at the tavern now.

Seemed like her idea to appeal to the tourists had worked. The place was jumping when we stepped inside, with two-thirds of the tables already full at barely past five. Awning windows lined three sides of the bar, and all of them were propped open to take advantage of the cross breeze off Pamlico Sound. The whole place screamed beach rustic, as it always had, but small touches here and there elevated the decor in some way I couldn't quite put my finger on. Fresh paint and fixtures maybe? It looked nice. Leveled up without being inaccessible to the locals. And Marv, the twelve-foot Marlin that was Ed's pride and joy, was still mounted above the bar, framed in Christmas lights.

Nice to see they'd kept the heart of the place.

Under Marv's watchful glass eyes, Bree herself —I assumed the tall, slim blonde with the take-no-shit attitude was Bree—moved behind the bar, filling glasses and chatting with locals, her grand-father at the other end doing the same.

We nabbed the last table by a window, and I plucked up a menu. "You wanna get an appetizer to go with our beers?"

"And risk Mom's wrath if we don't show up for dinner hungry? No, thank you."

"Since when have we ever shown up for a meal not hungry?"

"Not the point. She'll know. She always knows," he intoned.

One of the perks and downfalls of living on an island this small? There was no doing anything without everybody knowing about it. Engage in shenanigans at your peril because somebody was inevitably gonna tell your parents. I thought back to when I was about thirteen and I'd been caught trying beer for the first time. My dad had been waiting at home that afternoon, a fresh six-pack in hand. He'd made me drink the whole damned thing, then watched as I'd suffered the inevitable consequences and sicked it all back up again. I never knew who'd ratted me out.

I reached to tuck the menu back between the condiments and napkin dispenser and that was when I saw another blast from my past.

She still had the same glossy dark brown hair I remembered from high school, but she didn't hide behind it now. The mass of it was pulled up into one of those unaccountably sexy messy knots that left her neck and shoulders exposed. Little silver hoops winked in her ears, and the wash of sun off the sound lit her light brown skin with a golden glow. I itched to touch that skin, to see if my fingers came away covered in gold dust. And that smile. God. It wasn't even aimed in my direction, and it hit me straight in the gut. My gaze slid down her compact form, taking in the full breasts encased in a Brew House T-shirt and the narrow waist with a small apron tied around it. Shapely legs extended from denim cut-offs that framed an exquisite heart-shaped ass she *definitely* hadn't had in high school.

I'd always paid attention back then, watching out for her where I could because it was well known that her dad was a piece of shit and likely abusive. But I'd never seen anything actionable, and she'd been too young for me to do anything other than keep my distance.

She wasn't young now.

Drew twisted in his chair to see what I was looking at. "Ah. Guess you haven't seen her since she grew up."

"No. No, I haven't." I wished desperately that I already had a glass of water to wet my suddenly parched throat. "How's the family? I mean... after...?"

My question wiped the smirk off his face. "Not great. The police were never able to prove anything after Gwen disappeared. But the fact that Rios was the last person to see her alive means he's persona non grata around town. Without someone else to blame, there are plenty of folks who are happy to lay everything at his feet."

Rios. I remembered her brother. "He's still on-island?"

"Yeah."

"Why doesn't he leave?"

"Doesn't want to leave his sisters alone with Hector."

Right. Hector Carrera had always been a bad-tempered fucker. To my mind, the fact that Rios wouldn't leave his sisters unprotected was a weight on the side of his good character. But the public wanted a scapegoat. How had all that impacted the rest of them?

Before I could ask, a shadow fell over our table, and there she was. Damn if she wasn't ten times prettier close up.

"Welcome to OBX Brew House. I'm—"

"Caroline."

2

CAROLINE

He knows my name?

For a moment, I couldn't speak, as my inner teenage girl had heart palpitations. Lord knew she'd had hours—years, even—crushing on Hoyt McNamara.

Damn, but he'd grown up fine. And he'd been the handsomest boy I'd ever seen, even before he left. Those five years looked good on him, as did the extra width on his shoulders and thick muscles in his arms built from the labor of his job.

I'd known he was back on-island. In a community the size of ours, it was hard not to be aware of all the comings and goings, especially of one of the island's favorite sons. But I hadn't actually seen him since he returned to join the newly expanded fire department. Why would I? We'd never been friends. We'd never been anything. He'd just been the completely untouchable older boy who, so far as I'd known, hadn't even been aware I existed.

And yet he knows my name.

Shaking off the shock, I pasted on what I hoped was a proper professional smile instead of the lovesick puppy look I'd seen so frequently in the mirror back in high school. "Right. What can I get y'all?"

"Just a couple of beers. Thanks, Caroline," Drew said.

Drew. Right. Who'd been in the class below me and actually knew who I was. Mystery solved. They'd probably been talking about me, the same as everyone else in Sutter's Ferry. The idea of it chilled all those adolescent butterflies.

"Tap or bottle?"

They each made their requests, and I wove my way toward the bar, checking in on the rest of the tables in my section. A hefty portion of them were tourists. I always preferred the tourists. They had no idea who I was or who I was connected to. Which meant I didn't have to wonder what they thought when they looked at me, and I usually didn't have to worry they'd stiff me on tips. Those tips were the key that would grant me freedom, so I was motivated to earn as many as I could.

Bree caught me at the taps. "Well, well. Looks like Hoyt only got better looking with age."

I rolled my eyes, not bothering to dignify the remark with a response.

She leaned against the bar, a tray tucked under her arm as she watched the McNamara brothers across the room with sharp gray eyes. "What *is* it about firefighters that's so sexy?"

"Their willingness to risk life and limb to save other people. And the uniform." All true, though, that had never been the attraction of Hoyt for me.

"You should totally do something about that."

I waited for the foam to settle, then topped off each glass. "About what?"

"Locking down the new firefighter."

"I'm not interested in locking down anyone."

"Casual's good, too," Bree mused. "What's good for the gander and all that."

"I don't have time to date."

She laughed. "Who's talking about dating? I'm talking about having some fun. Fun would do you some good."

Fun? I didn't have time for that either. My one goal was to save enough money to move out of my father's house. My baby sister, Gabi, had finally graduated high school and would be leaving in the fall on a full-ride scholarship to UNC Chapel Hill. With her safely away, my brother and I would be free in a way we'd never been before because we'd both stuck in order to protect her. I was so damned close to being able to afford something of my own. Maybe not a lot of something, but anything was better than staying in the same house as *him*. Once I was safely out from under our father's thumb, maybe I'd be able to convince Rios to actually leave the island. His life here had been thoroughly ruined by a crime he hadn't committed. There was nothing left for him on Hatterwick. But I suspected he wouldn't budge unless I did, and I wasn't ready to leave the island, despite our father. This was home.

"Speaking of fun, when is Ford getting home?"

Ford Donoghue was a sure-fire means of changing the subject. While he was one of Rios's best friends, Bree and Ford had been practically joined at the hip since elementary school. She'd always been one of the guys. A position she'd never seemed to mind. But since I'd gotten to know her better the past few years working the bar, I'd started to wonder if there was something more there than friendship. She'd taken his leaving for college hard and the news of his college girlfriend even harder.

"His moms were in for lunch earlier. He's hooking up with Jace in Hilton Head. Then they're both coming home next week sometime."

Jace Hollingsworth was another of my brother's best friends, much to the disappointment of his parents. I suspected his dad especially hated how close Jace was to all the Wayward Sons—the nickname Rios and his friends had given themselves years before. As the son of a well-respected environmental attorney, the elder Hollingsworths tolerated Ford. But Rios, the son of a boat mechanic, and Sawyer Malone, progeny of a fisherman who spent more time in the bottle than on the water, definitely didn't pass muster. I loved Jace for thumbing his nose at his parents' snobbery and maintaining those bonds of forged brotherhood. That would be easier to do now. His parents had moved off-island a couple years ago, after Gwen Busby's disappearance and his sister Willa's near drowning. Other than Jace, I didn't think any of them had been back since then.

I loaded the drinks onto a tray. "Do the boys have big plans for the reunion?"

"I'm sure they do." The trace of resentment

lacing her tone suggested she expected them to ditch her.

I hoped they didn't. But I also knew the four of them had something together that didn't include Bree.

"Order up for seventeen and nine!"

Pivoting toward the pass-thru, I added the plates of food to my tray and headed back into the fray to deliver them. The crowd was getting thicker as more people came in from the beaches and whatever afternoon activities they'd pursued. I dropped off the orders and paused to take a few more before I made it back to the McNamara's table.

"Sorry for the delay."

Hoyt flashed a smile that had two deep dimples winking in his darkly stubbled cheeks. I ignored the way my stomach shimmied at those dimples. "It's no problem. Looks like it's jumping in here."

I cast a quick glance back at the restaurant, noting we were down to only two empty tables. "Gonna get worse before the night is through. Is there anything else I can get you?"

Before either man could answer, a male voice from a nearby table filled a momentary drop in the din. "Two years later and still no justice for that missing girl... almost like someone got away with murder here."

I recognized that snide voice. Chet Banks. Holding myself very still, I fought to keep my smile in place as the conversation continued.

"If it was up to me, that whole family would be run right off the island after what the boy did."

If I'd had any doubt that the McNamaras could hear, it was put to rest as I saw temper flare in Hoyt's green eyes.

"Supposedly, the cops didn't have quite enough to charge the brother. Tragic that no other evidence turned up." Marcus Hoffman. He wasn't usually a problem unless Chet was around to play ringleader.

"I catch even a whiff of that girl's bones washing up, and there'll be hell to pay."

Mortified and furious, I struggled to maintain my calm. They'd meant for me to hear. This was all intended to get a rise out of me. But I'd learned a long time ago that I should never respond. Responding just gave them more fuel.

But before I'd gathered my wits enough to repeat my question about whether the guys needed anything else, Hoyt was out of his seat, striding over to the table of assholes.

"You're out of line."

"Excuse me?"

"It's innocent until proven guilty where I come from. And, last I checked, guilt by association isn't a thing in this country. No one should be harassed for the accused crimes of family members when there's no proof or charges against them personally. Oh, that's right. There hasn't been proof or charges against her brother, either. It's unjust and unethical to spread blame without cause."

Chet huffed. "Unjust and unethical. Listen to this shit. Tell that to the dead girl's parents and see if they think it's unfair."

Hoyt didn't move, but I saw the stiffening of his posture and the twitch of the fingers that clearly wanted to curl into fists. I knew the signs, and I didn't know what to do with it. Apparently, his brother recognized it too, because suddenly Drew was there, too, forming a human wall between me and the other two men.

Hoyt's voice was quiet and level. "I'm sorry as can be for the Busbys' loss. But blaming innocent people for whatever happened to Gwen isn't gonna bring her back. Stop stirring the pot, Banks."

"Whatever. We can think what we want. Ain't no law against opinions."

"Then keep to sharing your fucking opinions in private."

"Or what?" At the combative tone, the restaurant fell almost silent.

"Or you'll have me to deal with."

What?

Ed Cartwright emerged from behind the bar looking like an extra from *Jaws* with his wiry gray beard and piercing blue eyes. "Banks, Hoffman, you're cut off for the day."

Chet puffed up. "We didn't do anything."

"You're being a dick, per usual. Out. Unless you want your drinking privileges permanently revoked."

With fulminating glares, Chet and Marcus rose from their chairs, draining their beers and stalking out. Not until they'd disappeared to the parking lot did I register I was shaking, my fingers clutching the order pad so tight, they'd gone white at the knuckles. Releasing a long, slow breath, I willed them to relax.

"You okay?"

I lifted my gaze to Hoyt, who'd stepped in front of me, effectively shielding me from the view of curious onlookers with his bigger bulk. All the temper was banked now, replaced with concern. He'd defended me. Defended my family. No one on Hatterwick did that. Well, not other than Rios's friends. Hardly anyone else dared go against the court of public opinion. But here was this man— my high school crush—doing exactly that after not seeing me for half a decade.

I had no idea what to do with that.

"Thank you. You just made a couple of enemies there."

Hoyt's shoulders twitched. "Couldn't call them anything else to begin with." His gaze continued to search my face, looking for... what?

Ed joined us. "Drinks on the house for you two. Caroline, take a minute."

"I don't need one—"

My boss fixed me with a steely glare. "Take a damned minute." He gave my shoulder a gentle squeeze, completely at odds with his hard tone. "Please."

With one last glance at Hoyt, I wove my way through the tables and disappeared through the swinging door into the kitchen, away from prying eyes. Inside, I dropped onto a stool in the corner.

Bree brought me a Coke. "Here. It'll help with the shakes."

I wrapped both hands around the glass lest I drop it.

"Looks like Hoyt's in the right profession."

"What?"

"Hero through and through. You should totally rethink your no dating policy."

I didn't answer, and she left me twisting in the whirl of my own thoughts.

Why had Hoyt done that? Just because it was the right thing to do? That was the kind of guy he'd been in high school, so I guessed he hadn't changed that much. But... why me? Why defend *me?* Did it mean something? Maybe I just wanted it to mean something because it had been so long since anyone outside my small circle had seemed to give a damn.

When I'd pulled myself together enough to go back to the floor, the McNamara brothers were gone, but I found an absurdly large tip left on the table. I pocketed the money and stared out toward the parking lot.

If I wasn't careful, that high school crush was going to turn into a brand-new grown-up version, one I suspected would be a whole lot bigger.

3

HOYT

"And what have we learned today?" I fixed Tim Jensen with a gimlet eye and waited.

The sixteen-year-old, who considered himself an amateur inventor, ran a hand through his singed hair. "That gunpowder measurements are important, and added shrapnel does not give a sparkly effect to a cannon blast."

I pressed my lips together to hold in a laugh. Since the kid hadn't actually gotten hurt with his homemade cannon experiment, the situation was kinda funny. But part of my job as a firefighter was to impress upon the teen that such experiments were not appropriate or safe. "And?"

Tim curled his shoulders forward. "And I shouldn't be trying to get ahead on next year's physics project about ballistics and mini explosions without adult supervision."

He shouldn't have been trying to make a cannon out of old pipes and a basic fuse system at all, but what teenage boy didn't, at some point, attempt to launch small projectiles at targets? For me and my friends, it had been a potato cannon. Plenty of boom, far less likelihood of actual fire or injury.

"Remind me to introduce you to the fine art of the potato cannon."

A car turned into the driveway, bumping far too fast along the rutted road. It had barely come to a stop beside the house before the drivers-side door opened and an older woman stumbled out, racing toward Tim. His mom, presumably.

"Oh, my God! What happened? Are you okay?"

I intercepted the panicked woman. "He's fine. I can't say the same for his cannon—"

"Cannon?" the woman shrieked.

"Tim, why don't you explain your experiment to your mom?"

The beseeching look the boy turned on me suggested that this was far worse punishment than anything else I could dish out.

Them's the breaks, kid.

Tim reluctantly recounted the decimation of his homemade cannon, which had shot backward when fired, blowing apart and spraying wires, pulleys, and timber supports across the yard, in addition to his "ammunition." Really, it was a miracle the kid hadn't lost an eye, or worse. I signaled to the rest of the crew to begin packing up. The assorted small grass fires his experiment had started had been effectively doused. By the time we were ready to go, Tim was grounded for the rest of his natural life.

As we rolled away from the Jensen house, Pete Novak grinned over at me from the driver's seat. "Bet this wasn't the kind of call you expected to be taking when you took a job back on-island, huh, L-T?"

"Not so much, no." After all the years coming up through the ranks in a big city fire department, I was accustomed to far more action. But I hadn't gotten into firefighting because I was an adrenaline junkie, so the idea of risking life and limb with slightly less frequency was more than a little appealing. The change certainly made my mother happy. "Any day that doesn't result in somebody getting hurt or losing everything is a good one in my book."

"I'll drink to that. Wanna hit up the Pelican to check it out after we get off shift? I've been hearing good things about their blackened shrimp."

"Nah, I've got a standing invite to my mama's for dinner. It'll be over by the time we're through with shift change, but she'll have made me a plate. Figure I'll go pick it up, then head home and crash. Another time."

"Holding you to it."

By the time we got back to the firehouse and did what needed doing, it was more than two hours past the end of my shift. Food I didn't have to make myself was definitely high on my list. I could do exactly as I'd planned and drop by Mom and Dad's for the inevitable leftovers. Or I could swing by the tavern for takeout and maybe get a few minutes of conversation with Caroline. I hadn't liked leaving as we had the other day, without knowing she was okay. But we'd had places to be and, as Drew had pointed out, there was nothing more I could reasonably be expected to do.

Not that either of those things had stopped me from thinking about her ever since.

We weren't friends. I doubt she even considered me more than a passing acquaintance in the same way ninety percent of islanders were. But I hadn't been able to get those rich, dark eyes out of my mind. There'd been hurt and frustration mixed in with the inevitable embarrassment. But there'd been fire, too. A desire to fight, barely leashed.

I chose not to analyze why I wanted to take on those battles for her. Maybe because I remembered the younger version of her who'd tried to make herself small. I'd always wondered if that was because she wanted to be less of a target at home. The possibility had never sat well with me. The idea that people other than her father were out to make her life difficult now was even harder to swallow. I wanted her to think of me as an ally. A friend. I told myself that was why I turned my truck toward OBX Brew House.

But the moment I stepped into the bar and spotted her, I knew I was lying.

She moved with ease and grace, a heavy tray full of food balanced on one shoulder. Her hair was bundled in another of those messy buns, though several curling strands had fallen by now, teasing the nape of that lovely neck I wanted to touch and taste. Yeah, my motives for being here definitely weren't purely altruistic. I was seriously attracted to this woman. Was she dating anybody?

I had no idea. It wasn't like I could ask such a question without cranking the rumor mill up to overdrive. But damn, I wanted to know if she was available, and if she was even interested.

If she was...

One thing at a time, McNamara.

At this hour, the kitchen wasn't too far from closing. As no one occupied the hostess station, I wove my way through tables and took a seat at the bar. No one else was behind it, and I didn't see any other servers. Was she here on her own? Only a handful of the tables were filled, and a quick scan of the room told me that most of the patrons were tourists, but still.

"You're too pretty to be working in a place like this, Caroline." The slightly slurred voice had my head whipping up from the menu.

Across the room, I spotted her straightening from refilling the man's water glass. I didn't have a clear view of him, but Caroline's body was ramrod straight, one hand curled around the edge of her tray so tightly I could see her white knuckles from where I sat.

"Will there be anything else for tonight?" Her tone was as stiff as the rest of her.

"What time do you get off, sweetheart?"

"Perhaps you'd like your check."

"Aw, now, don't be like that. You're always shutting me down. I just want to talk to you."

I was already out of my seat and closing the distance when I saw the guy reach out as if to touch her. I slid in between them, blocking his access. "Is there a problem here?"

Caroline's eyes flew to mine, and there was no mistaking the relief.

"This doesn't concern you, McNamara."

Recognizing Troy Lincoln, I made a snap decision and hoped Caroline would forgive me later. Shifting closer to her, I flashed a smile with sharp edges. "Well Troy, seeing as I'm pretty sure you're harassing my girlfriend, I'd say it does."

Troy's blond brows drew together. "She's not your girlfriend. You haven't been back but like a couple of weeks."

"Yep. And I know a good thing when I see one. Not gonna let it pass me by. You, however, are going to pass her by for the rest of the summer. And really for the rest of your life. She's not interested. And she's taken."

I didn't dare look at Caroline to see how she was reacting to this declaration. My entire focus was on the asshole who thought he was entitled to her time and attention. It wasn't the first time I'd seen him act like this. As the star pitcher for the high school baseball team, he'd earned a reputation back then for not taking 'No' for an answer. I had zero expectation that had changed since graduation, and I definitely wasn't going to stand by and let Caroline become his next victim.

Troy scowled and rose from his seat, stepping into my space. Given I had two inches and at least an extra thirty pounds on him, I wasn't intimidated. I just stared down my nose and waited. Several long, tense seconds ticked by before he evidently thought better of engaging and shoved past, shoulder checking me in the process. I pivoted and watched him storm out of the bar.

When I was sure he wasn't coming back, I turned to Caroline and found her staring at me with wide, dark eyes, the tray clutched to her chest like a shield.

Okay, so that wasn't how I'd expected this encounter to go.

I rubbed at the heat on the back of my neck. "Look, I apologize for going all caveman there, but he's not a guy who backs off just because a woman asks him to, and I got the impression this has been an ongoing thing."

With a slow exhale, she nodded, her shoulders

relaxing a little. "Ed normally shuts it down, but he's on the mainland for a doctor's appointment today, so I'm closing tonight. The other server on the schedule quit this afternoon, so I'm on my own, other than Jasper." She hooked a thumb toward the kitchen, so I assumed Jasper was the cook.

I didn't know a thing about Jasper, but all this said she had no one to back her up out here. "If it's all the same to you, I'm gonna stick around to make sure he doesn't bother you, and that he's not hanging around when you leave to give you any more hassle."

That flicker of surprise crossed her face again. Jesus, when was the last time someone other than me had done something kind?

"Thank you." She hesitated, frowning. "You realize what you told him is going to get all over the island, right?"

Had I registered that in the moment I'd claimed her? Sure. That had been the point. Did I regret it? Well, that depended on what she did with it.

"It doesn't bother me if it does. If you have a boyfriend, I suppose we should rectify that to make sure he doesn't want to put a fist in my face." As a fishing attempt, it wasn't exactly subtle, but when was the opportunity going to present itself again?

The corner of that full mouth quirked up. "No, no boyfriend. I don't date."

As good news went, I'd take it. Convincing her to take a chance on me would be easier than having to watch her with someone else.

"Well, if you change your mind on that, I'd love to take you out sometime. But that is one hundred percent not a condition of any of this. I want to make sure you're okay and not further harassed by that creep. If the illusion of being attached to me will achieve that, and you're okay with it, then so am I."

When she didn't immediately reply, I thought maybe I'd pushed too far.

"Why are you doing this?"

"Doing what?"

"This whole coming to my rescue thing? Again. At all. We barely know each other."

I considered saying something about how I had a thing for damsels in distress, but that didn't seem like the right direction. I shrugged. "Because it's the right thing to do."

If anything, my answer seemed to confound her more.

The sound of a male voice hollering, "Order up!" jolted her back into action.

"Did you want to order something? I assume you came in here for food."

"I did. Just got off shift. I thought I'd pick up something to go. But under the circumstances, I'll just eat here while you lock up."

"Sure. Kitchen technically closes in twenty minutes."

"Then have Jasper surprise me. Whatever's easy."

"You've got it. Grab a seat wherever."

I picked a table where I could watch the entrance, in case Troy decided to come back. The position also allowed me to watch Caroline as she finished closing out the remaining tables. I inhaled the blackened redfish and fries she brought me, then put myself to work, helping flip chairs on top of tables after she ushered out the last of the evening's patrons.

"You don't have to do that."

"I'm here. Might as well."

She didn't argue, and between the two of us, I hoped we managed to shut down a little quicker than she would've on her own. Jasper headed out as she was locking the main doors of the place.

Finally alone, I asked the question that had

been circling around my brain. "So, just for purposes of the gossip mill, are we or are we not dating? Again, it is completely fine if this is just an illusion for a while." My pride would get over it. Eventually. "I just want to be clear on our story."

No longer the focus of prying eyes, her guard dropped enough that I could see how tired she was. How much of that was the work and how much the burden of everything she carried?

"If you truly don't mind, it might alleviate a few problems. But I don't want to use you like that."

I'd love for you to use me in any way, shape, form, or fashion you like. "It's not using me since it was my idea. If I had a sister, I'd want someone to protect her, too."

"You're a good guy, Hoyt. I always knew that."

Score. But she hadn't actually answered my question yet about whether this was real or fake. Maybe she hadn't decided.

She locked the back door, and I walked her over to her car, a beat-up Chevy Malibu that had seen better days. Was that thing even roadworthy? I considered asking, then thought better of it.

"Just throwing it out there for consideration. In order to sell this, we're going to have to actually go out and be seen together. On dates. Why don't you let me take you to dinner, and you can decide after that whether you want this to be a relationship in name only for cover or if you'd be willing to date me for real?"

One hand on the car door, she stared at me again. I hoped that was surprise instead of horror.

"Are you serious?"

"Yeah." Because I definitely couldn't tell which end of the spectrum she fell on, I backpedaled. "Unless that makes you uncomfortable, in which case, we can just call it the name only and leave it at that."

Even in the poor light of the parking lot, I could see the blush rising in her cheeks. Both corners of her full lips curled up this time. "I'd like that. The dinner, I mean. And the chance to think about it. My next night off is day after tomorrow."

"It happens that's one of my nights off, too. So that's a plan."

"Is it?" That smile flickered again. "Don't we need a time and place?"

"We'll sort it out." It had been ages since I'd been on a first date, and the last ones hadn't mattered. I wasn't sure how I knew this one did, but I wasn't going to question it. "Get on home. Drive safe. I'll see you on Wednesday."

After one more brief hesitation, she slid into her car, which cranked without issue. Her brother had probably seen to that. Another plus in Rios's favor.

I watched her taillights disappear, resisting the urge to follow her. There'd been no further sign of Troy, and I had no reason to believe she wouldn't be fine. But as I stood in the empty parking lot, I couldn't quite shake the feeling of being watched.

4

CAROLINE

"A little bird told me you have a secret."

More than a little distracted, I locked the door behind me and turned to my baby sister. "And what might that be?"

Gabi grinned, her eyes sparkling. "That you're dating Hoyt McNamara."

Pure instinct prompted me to reach out to cover her mouth for quiet as I darted a glance back toward the house, even though I knew—I *knew*—Dad had already left for work. That swift kick of panic in my chest left me breathless.

Gabi dragged my hand away from her mouth, the smile gone. "Geez, Caro. I was just teasing. Mostly. I want all the details."

Exhaling a slow breath through my nose, I

herded her toward the car. "First, don't you dare speak a word of this around Dad. You know how he gets." There was a reason I didn't date, and his name was Hector Carrera. A fact I really should have considered last night when Hoyt came riding to my rescue. Again.

My sister slid into the passenger seat. "You're a grown adult. He doesn't have a say who you do or don't see."

Exasperated, I backed out of the drive. "You and I both know that so long as I live under his roof, it's his rules." No matter how ridiculous they might be. He needed to feel like he was in control. The head of the family. So far as he was concerned, what he said went. "Not that it matters, because I'm not dating Hoyt."

Gabi, ever the instigator, held up her phone. "Then why is everybody saying you are?"

I sighed, keeping my eyes fixed on the winding road that looped around the perimeter of the island to the vacation rental we were on deck to clean this morning. "Everybody? Who is everybody?"

"You know how the island is. Everybody." She started scrolling through her messages. "Lisa texted me first thing this morning. She heard from Derek, who was at the tavern last night when it all went down. Believe me, I want to hear more about *what* went down in a minute. And then Tara... she got it from Jasper's sister, Jenny."

The cracked vinyl of the steering wheel creaked under my tight grip as I recalled that there *had* actually been some locals in the bar during Hoyt's showdown with Troy. And Jasper... I'd thought he'd keep anything that happened at work to himself. "Great, so now Derek's spreading stories?"

Gabi shrugged. "Maisey called, too. She heard it from Edna at the post office. It's like wildfire."

Frustration soured the eggs I'd made for breakfast. Between the mother who'd left us when Gabi was only six, and Dad's abusive tendencies, which were one of the worst-kept secrets on Hatterwick, our family had always been the subject of island gossip. Then Gwen Busby had disappeared without a trace, and as the last person to see her alive, Rios had been wrongly accused of a crime he hadn't committed. No charges, no proof—there'd been no body, after all—but that didn't matter to the public at large. We'd been dodging whispers and stares ever since.

"And now they've got a new story to chew on," I muttered.

Gabi put down her phone, her expression softening. "Hey, it's just silly gossip. It's not like the stuff with Dad or... you know."

I knew she was trying to be supportive, but it was hard not to feel like just another character in the island's ongoing drama. "I know. It's just... tiring, you know? Being the subject of the latest rumor mill."

Her slight fingers curled around my arm in a squeeze. "I know. But hey, at least this time it's about something good, right? Hoyt's a catch."

I couldn't help but smile a little at her attempt to lighten the mood. "Yeah, I guess there's that. But we're not dating. He doesn't deserve to be dragged into our family's soap opera." And that was something I should've thought about last night before I'd agreed to dinner and even considering this insane plan.

"So you said. And yet everyone says otherwise. What exactly went down at the tavern, anyway?"

"Nothing." The answer was automatic, my desire to shield Gabi overriding everything else.

"Clearly, it was something. Try again, big sister."

"Just an entitled customer thinking I owed him my time outside of work. It was nothing I couldn't handle, but Hoyt overheard and intervened, announcing I was his girlfriend."

My sister clasped her hands over her chest, and I could practically see the hearts in her eyes. "That's so romantic."

Romantic wasn't quite the word I'd have chosen.

That Hoyt had stepped in to claim me as his without hesitation had filled me with more than simple relief and gratitude. His presence had given me an anchor in a situation that had spiraled beyond my comfort zone. But he'd slipped into the role so easily, his voice firm, his stance protective.

It had been an act. I'd known that. But for a fleeting moment, it had felt disarmingly real. His gaze had met mine in silent question or assurance, and in that split second, I'd felt a warmth I hadn't expected. A part of me had wondered what it would be like if it wasn't a ruse. If someone like him actually saw *me*. Beyond the gossip. Beyond the shadows of my family's past. To be wanted for who I was, not pitied for what I'd endured.

I'd shot that idea down in an instant as being ridiculous. Wanting such a thing, even knowing the fleeting daydream of it had been fueled by all those old teenaged fantasies about him, had brought on a sharp pang of guilt. I'd worked too hard to foster my own strength over the years. To be the one to handle what needed handling. To not need rescuing. I hated myself a little bit for being so comforted by having someone else take over, if only for a few moments. But God, I was so *tired* of all of it.

Then Hoyt had gone and announced he'd like to take me out for real. On a date. As if I were just some normal girl. And he'd compounded everything by saying his help wasn't contingent upon my saying yes. That it was just the right thing to do, to keep me safe. He'd put the decision about whether this relationship was real or fake entirely in my hands.

I'd thought about it all night, tossing and turning in my narrow bed. The man was temptation personified. A true-blue hero with ethics and heart and a noble streak as wide as Pamlico Sound. Then there was that body, hardened and honed by the labor of his job. I wanted my hands on it. Wanted to map every dip and curve of muscle. More, I wanted his hands on me. Imagining those work-roughened fingers trailing over my skin had left me so hot and bothered last night, I'd had to come out of the covers and lay beneath the faint breeze of the ceiling fan until the sheen of sweat had cooled and the urge to touch myself had passed. Such activities were for the privacy of the shower, not the room I shared with my sister.

I'd almost convinced myself I could give things with Hoyt a shot for real. God knew I wanted to. But so long as I still lived with my father, even fake dating him would be a problem. Not that I thought Dad actually had much of a chance of intimidating Hoyt, as he had the handful of guys I'd tried going out with in high school and after. But Dad wasn't the only problem. By aligning himself with me, Hoyt was likely to inherit some of the trouble that had stalked the rest of us. He deserved better. And that meant I couldn't have him. No matter how much high school me was throwing a conniption fit at the lost opportunity.

"Didn't you think it was romantic?" Gabi pressed.

"It wasn't real."

"But he came to your rescue, Caro! That means something."

"Yeah, it means he's a nice guy."

"Exactly! You deserve a nice guy."

"We both deserve a lot of things. Doesn't mean we're going to get them." Life had taught me that lesson in spades.

What we had, we'd worked and fought for. Gabi had busted her ass in school to earn that scholarship that was the ticket to a new life off island. Rios and I had stayed to see that she made it that far. What we'd do once she'd left was still up for debate. We'd both learned not to count our chickens, so until Gabi was safely at Chapel Hill, we were sticking to the plan. That plan was to keep our heads down and avoid doing anything that might prompt our father to fuck everything up for her.

"I think you're making a mistake. You've crushed on Hoyt forever."

I kept my face bland even as heat crawled up my neck. "Says who?"

"Says those old school notebooks where you doodled his name in hearts."

Why the hell hadn't I burned those?

"It was a long time ago."

"So you're saying you're *not* attracted to the sexy firefighter who came to your aid like a hero in a romance novel?"

"I'm saying we don't live in a romance novel, so I'm not expecting a happy ending."

"I bet a guy who looks like that is good at giving them," Gabi muttered.

"Gabi!"

"What? I'm eighteen, not ignorant. You totally deserve a boatload of happy endings."

Face flaming, I pulled into the driveway of the rental. "I'm not having this discussion."

"Ah ha!" She pointed at me in triumph. "That's proof that you *are* attracted."

"It's proof I'm breathing. Come on."

As I slipped out of the car, I couldn't shake the feeling of being on display, like some sort of spectacle for the islanders to gossip about, though I didn't actually see anyone around. This entire row of cottages was vacation rentals owned by the company that hired me to clean. But Gabi was right; at least this time, the story flying around was a relatively harmless one. To me, anyway. A far cry from the dark whispers that usually followed our family. But mine was the last name Hoyt's should be linked with.

Entering the code into the digital lock, I hauled my tote of cleaning supplies into the house and nearly dropped it. A wave of disbelief washed over me. The place was a disaster. The living room looked like the scene of a wild party—cushions were strewn across the floor, a couple of beer bottles had toppled over on the coffee table, spilling their contents onto scattered magazines. More empties were scattered around the room. In the kitchen, dirty dishes were piled high in the sink, food remnants caked and dried on plates and utensils. A faint, unpleasant odor of stale food and alcohol hung in the air, mixing with the musty scent of the sea. A trail of sandy footprints led from the front door through the hallway, as if the beach itself had been dragged in. The once pristine vacation home now resembled a college kegger, a stark contrast to the neat, welcoming oasis it was meant to be.

My heart sank at the sight.

Gabi stepped in behind me. "Holy shit. They aren't getting their deposit back."

"You've got that right. Let's get started. It's going to be a long day. I'm gonna be scrambling to finish this in time to make it to my shift at the tavern." But maybe by the end, I'd have figured out what to say to Hoyt when I rejected his kind offer.

5

HOYT

Boxes were everywhere. They seemed to multiply each time I glanced around the fixer-upper I'd had such burning ambition to renovate when I closed on the property. Now, standing amid the chaos of my stuff, the sheer scale of the project was finally sinking in. What had felt manageable in the abstract now loomed over me, a mammoth task that was going to take *years*. Not to mention money.

In the privacy of my kitchen—which didn't appear to have been updated since the nineteen seventies and was weirdly truncated because of how some previous owner had chosen to divide the space—I was willing to concede that I might have bitten off more than I could chew.

Not that I'd admit that to Drew on pain of death. I was the elder brother. The one who knew what he was doing. And I'd find my way with the house. Somehow. I just needed to pick a starting point. Make progress on something.

Maybe I could put together the Adirondack chairs I'd ordered to go up on the second-story porch so I could enjoy my coffee with the sun on my days off duty. After being in land-locked Raleigh all this time, that view of the ocean over the dunes on the other side of the two-lane coastal road wasn't something I'd take for granted. That was an improvement I could make before anything else. Though I had noted a faint spongy feel beneath my feet on both the upper and lower porches as I'd taken my initial tour of the whole place that told me I probably needed to move up replacing some porch boards first. After all the summers I'd worked construction growing up, I could do more than saw boards and hammer nails. That'd be an easy enough update. Certainly easier than updating the decorative elements like the porch frieze and gable trusses that were worn or missing after years of storms and neglect.

My gaze skimmed over the crumpled piece of paper in my hand, an attempt to list out the multitude of tasks ahead. Repair the roof. Replace the water heater on this side of the house. Knock out the dividing walls that had turned the place into a duplex. Check to see whether the plumbing needed upgrading. Not to mention the boatload of cosmetic projects like painting walls and refinishing floors. The list went all the way down the front and halfway down the back of the page, each item a reminder of the colossal amount of work that lay ahead. The one saving grace was that the electrical had been overhauled about ten years ago, so that was one major project I didn't have to take on.

I let the paper fall from my fingers, watching it land in a box labeled 'Kitchen Stuff'.

Unpacking. I should be unpacking. But every time I started, my mind wandered to the larger tasks, the structural changes, the renovations needed. I'd have to make some decisions about whether to try to mimic the original architecture or update it to something more simplistic or modern. Like the windows. By some miracle, many of those remaining were original, with twelve-over-twelve double-hung sashes. But those that had been replaced with more modern styles absolutely detracted from the historic charm of the place. Did I want to go for historical accuracy or efficiency? The cost of my electric bill by the end of the summer might decide me on that one. So long as they were still weatherproof, that was a project for Future Me.

And then, unbidden, my thoughts drifted to Caroline. Caroline, with that watchful gaze and hard-won smile that just made me want to work harder to earn it. Would she give me a chance to actually do that? Or would this relationship be in name only, lasting only long enough to deter would-be predators?

My phone vibrated with a text.

> Mom: Is there something you want to tell me?

"About what?"

As if she'd heard my reply, the little dots started bouncing.

> Mom: About you and a certain hard-working young lady?

No. She can't possibly have already heard about me and Caroline.

> Mom: You should bring Caroline to dinner.

I could ignore it. Pretend I was caught up in the work I was supposed to be doing. Or catching up on sleep. But that increased the chances she'd show up here in person to reiterate the invitation. I wasn't ready for her to see the state of the house. She'd worry, and I wouldn't hear the end of it until I finished renovations. At this rate, that'd be when I retired.

> Me: So y'all can interrogate her?
> No, ma'am. It's new. Leave it be.

That wasn't entirely a lie. And after our dinner tomorrow night, I hoped it would be the full truth. If Caroline elected to date me in name only, I could probably tell my family what was really going on. They'd support the fiction in the name of keeping her safe.

I watched the dots appear and disappear half a dozen times before the answer finally came.

> Mom: Sigh. Fine.

That would buy me a little time.

"Right. Unpacking." I could at least deal with my bedroom. There were few enough changes that would be happening in there. Paint, eventually, but I wouldn't tackle that until I had a clearer plan for the rest of the house.

No sooner had I dropped my phone into the pocket of my cargo shorts than it rang. Praying it wasn't my mother, I fished it out again.

It was Jamal Edwards, the officer on shift at the firehouse. "Hey Hoyt, I hate to ask, but can you cover for me for a few hours? My mama just called. She managed to crack the tank on the toilet while changing out the guts, and I gotta go help her deal with that before it gets any worse."

I hesitated, a part of me longing to say no, to focus on my own burgeoning disaster. But I couldn't. It wasn't in me to leave a member of my company in the lurch. "Sure, Jamal. I'll be there. Give me fifteen to get across island."

I hung up, a sense of relief washing over me, despite the unopened boxes and unfinished projects staring back at me. Right now, the job had to come first. If that gave me a reprieve from the overwhelming list of decisions I had to make, well, I'd call that a bonus for now. Maybe some distance would give me a little clarity.

Jamal was waiting outside when I pulled into the firehouse parking lot. "Thanks, man. I really appreciate this."

"No problem. Good luck with that toilet replacement. I hope the hardware store actually has one in stock."

"You and me both."

I braced myself for the inevitable ribbing as I pushed through the door, greeted by the familiar smell of strong coffee and the sound of easy chatter. If my mom had heard, there was no chance the rest of Sutter's Ferry FD hadn't. Gossip was usually a favorite firehouse pastime, tied with poker and cooking.

Smokey, the oldest of the crew, looked up from where he sprawled on the sofa. "Hey, if it isn't Lover Boy!"

Yep. I was in for it now. Because it was expected, I flashed a grin. "You guys never miss a beat, do you?"

Tank, built like his namesake and the powerhouse of our crew, propped his sock feet up on the coffee table. "So, when's the wedding? Got your tux ready?"

The room erupted in laughter. I shook my head, playing along. "Slow down. We're just having dinner."

"That's not what I heard." Quick on his feet and with his words, Flash gestured with a bottle of ginger ale. "What's the scoop, Hoyt? You and Caroline an item now?"

It was evidence of how long I'd been off-island that I'd so vastly underestimated how fast word of last night's encounter would spread.

"If they weren't before, I'd say they are now," Smokey added. "Word on the street is you got all kinds of possessive about your girl in front of Troy Lincoln last night."

The questions were nosy, but harmless—the kind of ball-busting that forged family ties and made long hours at the firehouse bearable. "We were keeping things on the down-low, but a public display seemed necessary. I know I've been gone a while, but I certainly didn't see any evidence that Troy has improved with age."

As I poured myself a cup of coffee, conversation shifted, the others sharing what they'd heard about Troy. All evidence that he was just as much of an asshole now as he had been at eighteen. I was hoping the subject had been effectively steered elsewhere, but Blaze, the youngest crew member, who I'd already figured out was the one looking to incite fires in any conversation, made the mistake of bringing it up again.

"You know, with her family history..."

Temper stirred. I hadn't thought anyone would be bold enough to bring up that garbage directly to me. It wouldn't do to lose my shit here, though, so I held up a hand and strove for some diplomacy. "Don't go there. Caroline's her own person. And as for her brother, I don't believe he had anything to do with Gwen Busby's disappearance."

There was a moment of silence, a sign of respect for my stance. I appreciated that they seemed to know when to back off. This was the kind of thing that could absolutely damage the camaraderie of the team, and we couldn't afford that. Out on the job, we depended on each other to stay safe and alive.

I took a sip of my coffee, my mind wandering to Caroline. She was strong, resilient, and had been through more than her fair share of trouble, thanks to the island's rumor mill. I admired her for it. And despite the gossip, I was looking forward to spending some real one-on-one time with her, to see where things could go if she'd only give us a chance.

The alarm shattered the afternoon calm, catapulting us all into action. The banter, the teasing, the heavy cloud of gossip, all evaporated as we leapt into coordinated action. In the midst of the controlled chaos, a small part of me couldn't help but feel grateful for the interruption. It was a reminder of why I'd come back to Hatterwick—to make a difference, to be part of this brotherhood.

The fire was on the Atlantic side of the island, along the row of houses that had fallen to investors who were more interested in making vacation rentals than homes. As we approached, an ominous cloud of smoke billowed into the sky, a stark contrast to the peaceful backdrop of beach and ocean. A visibly shaken couple stood well back from the blaze as the engine rolled to a stop. The next booking or owners? Either way, they were likely the ones who'd called it in.

With Jamal out, it was on me to take command. It was a role I'd trained for, even if this was my first time out in this capacity with this department. The responsibility of command meant overseeing the safety of not just the structure and its occupants, but my crew as well.

"Is anyone inside?" I shouted.

The man wrapped an arm around his companion. "We don't know. We spotted the smoke when we got here."

I scanned quickly for other vehicles but saw only the car the couple must have arrived in. "Let's get a line on that fire in back. Flash, head in through the front and check for anyone inside."

My team sprang into action, efficiency and urgency in every step. Tank and Smokey started unrolling the hoses, while Flash and I quickly donned our breathing apparatus.

"Everybody look alive. It doesn't look too bad yet, but we all know this can turn on a dime."

Flash kicked in the front door and hustled inside, and the rest of us moved around to the back. The fire hadn't made it to the wooden deck yet. Hose in hand, I pounded up the steps and made for the back door, breaking my way inside. The heat in the smoke-filled kitchen hit like a physical force, a wall of searing air that threatened to push me back. I gripped the hose, directing the water at the base of the flames, the most effective point of attack. The fire was stubborn, devouring the wooden cabinets and kitchen fixtures.

"Get another line in here. Keep the water on it!"

The crackling of the flames and the hiss of steam as water met fire filled the air, a chaotic symphony as familiar as my own name. I kept a wary eye on the ceiling, mindful of potential structural damage. It was a constant calculation as we fought to contain, then extinguish the blaze.

By the time the fire was finally doused, the structure was mostly intact, but the kitchen was devastated. As outcomes went, it was a hell of a lot better than it could've been.

"Hey L-T, come look at this."

Following Smokey's gesture, I examined the mess of what used to be the stove. What had once been a plastic bin of—something—had melted to the top. Evidence of assorted containers was inside. The burn pattern suggested this was the point of origin.

"Accident or incendiary?" Smokey murmured.

In my years as a firefighter, I'd seen all kinds of idiot moves. Setting a cleaning caddy on a stove that was still hot was well within the realm of possibility. But something about this was raising my internal alarms. "Too soon to say."

"L-T, the owner is here."

I followed Tank outside, where a middled-aged guy stood at the edge of the perimeter we'd established, one arm folded over his chest, the other braced behind his head as he stared at the house in horror.

"I'm Lieutenant McNamara. You're the owner?"

"Yes. Jim Foster. How bad is it?"

"Not a total loss, but you're out a kitchen for sure." I didn't mention the additional damage from our suppression efforts. "Once we clear the house, we'll need to investigate to determine the cause of the fire. You'll need our report for your insurance."

"How long will that take?"

"I can't give any estimates on that at this time. We're going to need to know who had access to the house."

Foster speared a hand through his wiry gray hair. "Sure. Of course. The last renters left early this morning."

"You have some names?"

"The registration was to a guy named Lucas Platt. I'd have to pull the records to see who else was supposed to be here with him. Bachelor party. My cleaning crew said they left the place a total wreck."

"So the cleaning crew has been in since they left?"

"Yeah. Got here this morning around ten, I think."

"Anybody since then?"

"Not so far as I know."

"Right. And the name of the cleaners?"

"Caroline and Gabi Carrera."

I barely held in my jolt of surprise at hearing Caroline's name. I had to stay focused. There were procedures to follow, and it would be essential that I stick to them exactly.

The fire was out, but it seemed the aftermath was just beginning.

6

CAROLINE

Unable to shake the itch between my shoulder blades, I scanned the tavern. As it was just after five on a Tuesday, the crowd was more heavily local, though there were still plenty of tourists mixed in. It was those locals who had me ill at ease. After everything that had happened this past week with Chet and Troy, I kept waiting for the other shoe to drop.

How many more scenes would Ed tolerate before he cut me loose? They weren't my fault. Not exactly. And he'd always been supportive and understanding. But if his business was hurt, I wouldn't be able to blame him. I needed this job, just like I needed all the other side gigs I could pick up.

I took drink orders for a table of six and headed back for the bar. A familiar figure was perched on a stool toward the end. His sandy hair needed a trim, as did his stubbled cheeks. But he didn't look too bad, all things considered.

I closed the distance and wrapped an arm around his shoulder in a half hug as I tipped my head to his. "Are you here to raise a glass in memory of your dad, or are you hanging out to keep an eye on me?"

Sawyer's arm slid around my waist and squeezed. "Is it that obvious?"

"You haven't been in since the funeral." Not surprising. More often than not, the whole reason Sawyer had come in had been to retrieve his father from the bar. This place had to be full of memories for him.

"Rios mentioned the trouble you had the past week. We didn't think it would be a bad thing for one of us to keep an eye out, and he's tied up on a job."

It wasn't the first time my brother had asked one of his friends for an assist. I didn't mind. All three of them were like other brothers to me. With Ford and Jace gone off to college, that meant Sawyer was the only one left.

He pivoted toward me, and I noted humor

mixed with the grief in his eyes. "Though, from what I hear, you've got an ally we hadn't counted on."

Hoyt. Shit. Had my brother already heard we were "dating" or only about the two confrontations?

Yep, definitely wasn't touching that one with a ten-foot pole. If Sawyer was here for recon, he wouldn't be getting more info from me.

I stepped away from him and moved behind the bar. "The situations got handled." I set glasses beneath the taps and began to fill the order. "What about you? How are you holding up?"

Those lanky shoulders jerked in a shrug. "It's been two months. I keep expecting to come home and find him nodded off in his recliner with a bottle of Jim Beam on the table."

With the death of his father, Sawyer was all on his own. His mom had died in childbirth trying to bring a baby girl into the world when he was only seven. The baby hadn't made it either, and Hank Malone had never recovered from the loss. He'd fallen into the bottle and hadn't come back out, so Sawyer had been forced to grow up fast. Hank hadn't been a mean or problematic drunk. Hadn't been a bad guy. He'd just been utterly heartbroken and hadn't had the strength to pull himself together for the son who'd remained.

Because I knew Sawyer wasn't likely to want a beer, I automatically filled a glass with the root beer he preferred. As I set it in front of him, I wondered what it was like to love someone so much that their loss absolutely broke you. Gabi, with her miraculous romanticism, would no doubt find it terribly swoon-worthy. I wasn't so sure I wanted to feel that deeply. That kind of love opened you up to the potential for incredible loss. I had no desire to give anyone that kind of power over me.

The front door opened, and I glanced automatically, mentally measuring the size of the party against the available tables. But my brain short-circuited as I spotted Hoyt striding in, dressed in his uniform of cargo pants and a navy SFFD T-shirt. He'd shaved the scruff for work, so there was nothing hiding the view of that strong jaw. My traitorous heart lurched with a nauseating combination of joy and dread. I'd promised myself that when I saw him again, I'd talk to him about why this whole relationship thing—be it fake or otherwise—was a terrible idea.

But I wasn't ready yet. I hadn't thought I'd need to have this conversation until dinner tomorrow.

Then I registered he wasn't alone. The fire

chief, Michael Thompson, was with him. So maybe they were here for dinner for a work thing?

Hoyt caught my eye and flashed a smile that seemed a little strained around the edges. When they headed in my direction, my palms went damp. Everything about the two of them shouted "Bad news!"

My brain frantically ran through what the problem might be. During shifts, my phone stayed in my locker, so if anyone had tried to reach me about an emergency with one of my siblings, they'd have had to call the tavern directly. I hadn't heard the phone ring, and nobody had come to get me. But the fire department frequently took medical calls on the island, so what if this was them coming to notify me in person?

Hoyt stopped at the edge of the bar. "Hey, Caroline."

I surreptitiously wiped my hands on a bar towel, then kept it in my hands to squeeze as the anxiety cranked up to eleven. "Hey. What's going on? Is everything okay? Is it Gabi? Rios?"

He lifted his hands, palms out. "Shit. No. We didn't mean to worry you. Nobody's hurt."

I loosed a breath. That was something. But then, why were they here?

"We just need to ask you some questions," Chief Thompson added.

Questions? About what? If the chief was here, this was something in an official capacity. The anxiety came roaring back as I tried to imagine what any of this had to do with me.

From his perch at the bar, I sensed Sawyer tense, waiting for action himself.

Chief Thompson's eyes were kind. "We can tell you're busy. We can wait for a little bit, but the questions we have shouldn't take too long if you can find a stopping point."

"I..." I looked at the tray of waiting drinks. "Just a minute." I flagged down Tracy, one of the other servers on shift. "Can you take this out to table twelve?"

"Sure."

I tried to ignore her look of blatant curiosity as she lifted the tray and headed out.

Ed closed in from the other end of the bar. "What's going on?"

"Nothing bad. We just need to have a few words with Caroline."

What did it mean that Hoyt was no longer talking?

"Y'all can take it back to the office for some privacy," Ed offered.

Bless the man. I squeezed his arm in gratitude as I led the two firefighters through the kitchen door, away from prying eyes. The office was a tiny, square room, with barely enough space for a battered metal desk and a couple of chairs. By the time we crowded inside, the nerves were strong enough to make me shake.

"Go on and have a seat. Make yourself comfortable." Chief Thompson's words and tone were kind, but I recognized an order when I heard one.

Because there wasn't anywhere else to go, I circled behind the desk and dropped into the rolling office chair. It gave a resounding squeak of protest and tipped back so fast I nearly got thrown into the wall. With a yelp, I grabbed onto the desk to steady myself.

Hoyt flashed a smile that was probably meant to be reassuring. "Looks like Ed needs to get some new office furniture."

"We don't spend much time in here, as a rule. What's going on?"

Chief Thompson took the only other chair. "Were you at 1487 Sandpiper Road earlier today?"

I blinked. "Yeah. I do cleaning for Shoreline Rentals. I was turning it over for the next round of guests coming in today. Why? What happened?" Except I knew. Because why else would the fire department be here in an official capacity?

"There was a fire there this afternoon."

"Oh, my God. Was anyone hurt?" I tried to think what time the renters were meant to be coming in.

"No. Nobody was inside." Hoyt perched on the edge of the desk because there was nowhere else for him to sit. "The next tenants were the ones who called in the fire, actually. Everybody's okay."

Good. That was good. "The house?"

Hoyt winced. "It's less okay. But it didn't burn to the ground."

I covered my mouth. "Oh, God."

Chief Thompson picked up the thread again. "I'm sure this was a shock. Mr. Foster mentioned you and your sister do the cleaning?"

"Yes."

"Was she with you today?"

"I—yes."

"What time did the two of you arrive?"

I took them through it, answering an array of questions about the condition of the house, what time we'd left.

"We finished up around one because I had to be here for work at one-thirty. I had just enough time to drop Gabi off at a friend's before I came in for work. You can see my time card by the back door where I clocked in."

"That's fine, and we'll do that." The chief made some notes on a little pad. "When you go on your cleaning jobs, do you use products already in the house or do you have one of those little tote things to carry around your stuff?"

"I have a tote. Some of the houses have supplies, but I don't rely on them being up to date. Sometimes the guests will take them. Why they'd want a bottle of Windex as a vacation souvenir, I have no idea."

"Do you still have yours? Or do you think you could have left it at the house?"

I frowned. Where was he going with this? "No, I have it. It's in my car. Why?"

"Can we go check to make sure it's there for sure?" Chief Thompson asked.

Fresh anxiety spooled in my belly. This sounded a hell of a lot like they were working their way toward an accusation. Without a word, I rose and scooted past them, leading both men out the back door to the employee parking lot. My hands were shaking as I popped the trunk, terrified of what I might see. But the bright blue tote was still there, each of the bottles lined up like soldiers along both sides.

Beside me, Hoyt relaxed.

"Did your sister have a second one?" Thompson asked.

"No. We just have the one. Frequently, it's just me. She only helps on weekends and in the summer. Seriously, what is going on here?"

The fire chief offered a kind smile. "We're just trying to get to the bottom of that to see if what happened was an accident or on purpose."

I swayed as all the blood drained from my face. "You don't think that I—"

"No." Hoyt's voice was firm. "There's no reason to think you had anything to do with this. We're just following up leads and crossing off possibilities. There was something melted on the stove that appeared to be the point of origin. We're just trying to figure out what it was. We thought it might have been a bin of cleaning supplies that could have accidentally been left there. But yours is here, so everything is fine."

Everything definitely wasn't fine. A house I'd cleaned had burned. From the sound of it, Gabi and I were the last ones inside it. What if Mr. Foster fired us over this?

I scooped a hand through my hair. "My boss..."

"Mr. Foster. What sort of relationship do you have with him?"

"I mean, we don't have much of one. I've been cleaning his vacation rentals for a few years now. He gave me a chance when a lot of people wouldn't, and he pays fairly. I have no reason to want to hurt him." I couldn't stop myself from looking at Hoyt. "That's what this is about, right? Looking to see if I have a motive?"

It was Thompson who answered. "It's just part of the process to ask. Foster also reported you have a good working relationship and that you're very conscientious. He has no reason to blame you for this."

I blinked back a sudden rush of tears. Chief Thompson was a gruff but fair man. He hadn't had it out for our family in the way a lot of other people on the island had. "Thank you."

He offered a business card. "That's all we've got, for now. If you remember anything, please let us know."

"Of course."

"We'll let you get back to work. McNamara?"

"I'll be along in just a few, Chief."

As the older man walked away, I wished like hell I had something to do with my hands. Because this was it. This was the part where Hoyt backed out of the agreement he never should've offered in the first place. Which, great, then I didn't have to be the one who came across looking ungrateful or whatever. But damn, it still felt like I was being dumped, and the whole thing hadn't even been real.

Before I knew what was happening, Hoyt pulled me in for a hug. It wasn't tight or long, not overly familiar, but it lit up every inch of my body where it pressed against his. He smelled of some woodsy body wash and sea air. God, he smelled good. It took everything I had not to bury my nose against his throat and sniff. Instead, I accepted this for the friendly comfort it was meant to be. Maybe he was letting me down gently.

With one last little squeeze, he stepped back. "I just wanted to say sorry for having to bring that all up into your workplace. Nature of the job. And I'm really looking forward to tomorrow night."

Wait... what?

But he wasn't looking at me with revulsion or suspicion.

"Are you sure that's still a good idea?"

"Absolutely. I'm cooking. Under the circumstances, I thought you might appreciate not being paraded in public."

It's not over.

Which was absolutely stupid of me to think about when I was the one who planned to end this farce before it went any further. But yeah, having that conversation in private would be better.

"That's really thoughtful of you."

He flashed those dimples. "I'm a thoughtful guy. I can pick you up—"

"No. No, I'll meet you." The last thing I needed was my father catching wind of this, if he hadn't already. "Where?"

Hoyt reeled off an address and a time and began walking backward. "I gotta get back to work, but I'll see you tomorrow."

I lifted a hand in a reluctant wave. "Tomorrow."

7

HOYT

The prospect of having Caroline over to the house for dinner lit a fire under my ass in a way nothing else had. Having anybody over hadn't been on my radar for a while, but after that whole scene at the tavern yesterday, I knew people would be talking, and it was more important to me that she be comfortable. So I spent most of the day unpacking the bare essentials, corralling the rest, and obsessively cleaning the first floor. I even made a trip to Beachcomber Bargains, the island thrift store, to see if I could scrape up a little more furniture. I'd brought very little with me from Raleigh, where my roommates and I had leased a furnished apartment. The kitchen table and chairs I found had seen better days, but, like the house, they had good bones. Down the line, I'd strip and refinish them. For tonight, they'd give us a more adult place to sit than the gaming chairs and futon that made me feel like the confirmed bachelor I'd been for longer than I cared to think about.

On the drive back out to the house, I'd impulsively stopped to pick a clutch of wildflowers from the side of the road. I put them in a Mason jar I managed to scrounge up and set the whole thing in the middle of the table. Before I could decide if it looked charming or just trashy, the doorbell rang.

Shoving down uncharacteristic nerves, I wiped my hands on my shorts and answered the door, which stuck. Because, of course, it did. With a little lift of the knob and a heave-ho, I managed to drag it open.

Caroline stood on my dilapidated porch looking as beautiful as ever. But I noted a hint of nerves that mirrored my own in the way her fingers gripped the strap of her purse. She'd left her hair down tonight. The long, mink-brown waves of it cascaded over her shoulders and down her back. My fingers itched to bury themselves in the thick mass to see if it was as silky as it looked. The golden brown skin left exposed by the little sundress she wore seemed to glow in the lowering sun. The sight of those little spaghetti straps made my fingers itch to nudge them down so I could explore every inch with my mouth. Her dark eyes, usually so full of resolve and quiet strength, held hesitancy tonight, as if she was wrestling with a decision she hadn't quite made. Maybe she was still on the fence about this real or fake dating thing.

Don't screw this up, McNamara.

Flashing a smile, I stepped back. "Hey. Come on inside. Sorry about the mess. I'm still moving in and haven't finished unpacking. I just closed on the house a couple weeks ago."

Dear God, stop babbling.

"It's fine. I'm not fussy." But her gaze tracked over the entryway.

What did she see? The wear and tear from all the years of neglect or the gems hidden beneath it?

"The place has good bones." Her fingers trailed over the newel post of the stairs. "Needs some TLC, but the best houses always do."

Something in me relaxed. "My sentiments exactly. Come on back."

I led her through the house to the kitchen, which was the most put-together room by far. The flash of her smile at the sight of the flowers made me relax a little more. They hadn't been a bad call.

Caroline hung her purse on one of the chairs. "What smells so good?"

"Well, I'm not ashamed to admit that I adhere to the firefighter stereotype. I'm an excellent cook. What you smell is my famous arrabbiata sauce." To give myself something to do with my hands, I lifted the lid and stirred. "I hope you're okay with pasta."

"Pasta of all kinds is a staple in our house. We rotate dinner duty, and it's something all three of us could cook from a very young age."

"Seems fair. Wine? It's a classic chianti." I was no connoisseur, but that had seemed a safe enough bet with a red sauce.

"Sure. Thanks."

I uncorked the bottle and poured into a couple of jelly jars. "I do actually own wine glasses—" I was pretty sure, at least. "But I haven't found them yet."

Caroline's lips curved. "I'm not a woman who stands on formality. And I'm pretty sure we *don't* own wine glasses at our house, so..."

I passed her a glass and lifted my own. "*Salute.*"
"*Salute.*"

"So, how are you doing?" I didn't specify with

what. We both knew that yesterday's questioning had already hit the island gossip train. I hadn't wanted to do it at her job for exactly that reason, but my personal sympathies couldn't overrule the investigation.

"I'm doing okay."

I wasn't sure I believed it, but I decided to take her at her word. I wanted to spend some uncomplicated time with her, and bringing up the stresses she was constantly under definitely wasn't the way to accomplish that.

Lifting the lid on the pot, I gave the sauce a stir. "You know, I remember you from high school."

I turned just in time to catch her epic wince. She took a hefty sip of her wine. "Well, that's mortifying."

"Why? I remember you as being quiet and studious. I always wondered what was going on in that brain of yours."

"Why would you remember me at all? You were well ahead of me. A senior to my freshman."

The sides of the jar were smooth as I rolled it between my fingers. "I made it a point to watch you." When her brows nearly hit her hairline, I rushed on. "Not in some kind of creepy stalker way, but just... My dad works with your dad down at the boatyard, and your dad has a reputation. I worried about you. About all three of you. Especially after your mom—" I cut myself off as pink rose in her cheeks.

She didn't meet my eyes as she set her glass down.

Way to go, McNamara. How's that foot taste?

Feeling like I'd blown my shot already, I reached out to lay a hand over hers on the table. "I don't say that to embarrass you. I just wanted to let you know that my looking out for you isn't a new thing."

Her head snapped up from where she'd been staring at my hand, and her expression was full of baffled surprise. "I appreciate that. I think. It's been a long time since anybody other than my brother and his friends really looked out for me."

Given everything I'd overheard about Rios since I got back, I wasn't surprised. "For the record, I don't believe your brother did anything. It's really shitty that people are trying to hold him accountable just because they don't have someone to legitimately blame."

"Thank you."

Because she hadn't moved since I touched her, I eased back. "So, moratorium on the shitty stuff. Tell me about something good in your world."

God, I hoped there was something, otherwise I'd really just stepped in it.

Caroline picked up her glass again and sipped. "My baby sister has a full-ride academic scholarship to UNC Chapel Hill. She'll be leaving for college at the end of the summer."

"Shit, that's a great school. Full-ride there is no joke."

"Gabi's brilliant." The smile that curved her lips made it crystal clear that she was as proud of her sister as any parent.

"That'll be different, having her off island."

"It will give Rios and me some more flexibility. I'll *finally* be able to move out of our father's house. I've just got to find a place I can afford."

And here I was with a duplex. Trying to keep it casual, I sipped my wine. "What's your budget?" Not that it mattered. I'd rent to her at a rate she could afford if she was actually interested in the other unit. It was the first time I'd ever been in a position to really *help* her escape the situation with her father.

"Why?"

"Because this house is a duplex. I need to find a tenant for the other half." Of course, that hadn't been the plan at all. But this was Caroline.

She shook her head. "I couldn't do that to you."

I wasn't sure what she thought she'd be doing. "You'd be helping me out. I'd intended to fix the place up first, but as you've no doubt clued in on, I don't have a ton of extra time, and I'll be spending it on this side first. C'mon, let's take a look."

Before she could protest, I set down my wine and nudged her toward the front door. We stepped outside, into the balmy summer evening, and circled around the lower level porch that followed the asymmetrical facade of the house to the other door. One of the few things I had managed in the past week was replacement of some rotten floorboards out here and upstairs, where I'd noted I needed to replace some railing, too. I let us into the unit and flipped on the lights to show the kitchen. As I hadn't intended to come over here, it hadn't been cleaned yet, so I focused on the high points.

"The floors eventually need refinishing, but they're solid. Original oak. The cabinets aren't what you call pretty, but again, solid."

"Nothing a little paint wouldn't fix," she murmured.

"Or a lot of paint. The walls need a fresh coat throughout."

I took her through the living room in the back corner and the other smaller room that might serve as an office or other bedroom, then up the converted service stairs to the second floor.

"There are two bedrooms up here that share a full bath. The layout is a little funky because whoever converted this place legit carved up a normal house, but it's objectively solid, the roof doesn't leak, and you'd know your neighbor at least a little bit."

I could see her reluctant interest and went in for the kill, naming a ridiculously low price I prayed she could afford.

She shot me some major side eye. "You're massively underpricing."

I totally was, but I shrugged. "I got this thing in a short sale and paid a stupid low price for it. Between rent and, if you want to take on the painting to fix up this side yourself, I think we can call it even. We could even do things on a month-to-month basis, if that's more comfortable for you."

She studied me for a long minute. "Is this just another way to save me?"

I sensed I'd lose all traction with her if I wasn't completely honest. "Maybe some. But I truly do need a tenant. Having someone who'd fix up this side would save me a lot of time and effort. And also, if you're here, I can keep an eye out for you, whether we decide the dating thing is real or not."

The floor creaked as she paced across the room to the window that faced the water. From this position, you could just see the expanse of it over the dunes.

"I came over here tonight to save you from yourself and tell you thanks, but no thanks to your kind offer of fake dating me. You don't need all the stress and headaches that being linked to me in any way would cause you."

"I'm a big boy. One who doesn't give a shit what other people think."

"That's easy to say when you haven't had to deal with the consequences of being attached to me yet."

"Whatever they are, it's a price I'm willing to pay. I like you, Caroline. And I want to be someone who's in your corner, in whatever way you're okay with."

With a half laugh, she turned and waved a hand at me. "See? You say stuff like that, and it makes it really hard not to want to date you for real."

I held in the fist pump, but not the smile. "I'll keep that in mind. But we're not talking about the status of our relationship just now. We're talking business."

She caught her lower lip between her teeth,

and it was all I could do to keep my focus on the conversation rather than wanting to do the same with my own teeth. If she said yes to this, there was a strong possibility that her answer to the rest would be no. And she needed to know that was an option, no matter what I really wanted long term.

"Listen, my renting to you is entirely unrelated to the rest of it. You need a place. I have a place. One that's got room for all three of you and is available as soon as I can get to the hardware store to have keys made. Do you want it?"

8

CAROLINE

"I can't believe you signed a lease without talking to us first."

I ignored my brother's implied criticism and led my family up the steps of the two-story beach house that would now be home, trailing a hand over the wood railing smoothed by time and tidal winds. As most houses on Hatterwick, this one sat up on brick piers, elevated several feet above ground level to allow room for flooding. It was a necessary architectural choice here on the Outer Banks of North Carolina. The cedar shake siding was faded to the color of driftwood from decades of salt air. It would need some patching where moisture had caused the wood to rot and shingles to loosen, but Hoyt would see to that. The brickwork on the two chimneys marking either end of the steeply pitched gable roof was crumbling in spots. That might actually be a bit outside the range of home improvement projects he could tackle himself, but there'd be someone on-island who could handle it. Probably.

Using the keys Hoyt had dropped off yesterday, I opened the apartment and led my siblings inside. "It was a really good deal. I had to make a fast decision or someone else was going to get it."

That wasn't strictly true. I was pretty sure that Hoyt would have waited as long as I needed to make the decision. But it seemed like a better answer to my brother than admitting the truth—that I had been impulsive.

As a rule, I was never impulsive. Impulsive meant costly mistakes and trouble. But here was my own personal hero, putting himself out there again to give me exactly what I needed. If I hadn't said yes, it would've likely been another few months before I was able to afford something. And then who knew how long it might have taken to find anything open? The prospect of getting away from my father immediately was too appealing to second guess.

Rios and Gabi trailed me inside. "What did you agree to pay for this place?" I could hear the underlying tone in his voice that indicated he wasn't impressed with what he saw.

I told him the rate Hoyt and I had agreed upon. "Month-to-month, without the requirement of last month's rent or an additional deposit."

Suspicion darkened Rios's face, his dark brows drawing down in a forbidding scowl. "Why would he rent the place for that cheap? Even in this condition, he could get three times that in the current market."

At that reminder, I squashed the sense of guilt that had been dogging me since I'd accepted Hoyt's more than generous offer. At least the one about the apartment. "He said he got it on a short sale, so he doesn't have to charge as much. And part of the deal we made is that I'll do the painting and fixing up myself. I totally support that, since it means I'll have more control over things. It will be nice to have a space of my own that I can decorate and make a home."

Certainly our father's house hadn't actually been home since our mother left twelve years ago. No amount of good intentions could make up for the anger and bitterness that had soaked into those walls since Mama had walked out without a word, leaving us all behind. This place would be a fresh start for all of us.

"Are you sure that's all you're expected to pay?"

I tore my brain away from contemplating cabinet colors. "What do you mean?"

My brother leveled me with hard eyes and an even harder jaw. "Is he using this to strong-arm you into dating him?"

For a long moment, all I could do was stare at him. "Wow. This is what you think of me? Of him? You really can't imagine a scenario in which he might actually want to date me, and I might actually want to date him back?"

Rios's expression softened. "I didn't mean it like that. But you don't date. And suddenly this guy is back on-island, and you're moving into the other half of his duplex, and everybody says you're dating. You can't blame me for asking questions."

No, I couldn't blame him for that. Rios hadn't exactly been a trusting guy before the shit went down with Gwen Busby's disappearance. Since then, his natural suspicions of everyone's motives had been dialed up to eleven.

I'd known the rumors about me and Hoyt would've reached him well before now, and I supposed I ought to have been grateful I hadn't had to deal with this sooner. Grateful, too, that he hadn't confronted Hoyt directly. After everything he'd been through, he hard a hard time believing that there was anyone outside his circle on this island who didn't want to hurt us.

"You know why I don't date. Moving away from Dad alleviates a big part of that. Either way, Hoyt is a good man. He's stepped in on more than one occasion to defend me when he didn't have to. He's gone out of his way to make it clear that his help and this lease have nothing to do with whether I choose to date him for real or not."

Rios frowned. "What do you mean, for real?"

I blew out a long breath. I hadn't meant to say that. "Part of that stepping in was pretending to be my boyfriend in front of Troy Lincoln. After that, he basically said that we could fake date to keep the creeps away. But he'd like to date me for real." And dammit, I wanted to date him for real, too. I wanted to believe this connection I felt could be the start of something. But I hadn't decided yet.

"Why wouldn't you date him for real? He's totally acting like a knight in shining armor, and he clearly cares for you." My sister insisted.

"He doesn't know her well enough to care yet."

The glare I shot at Rios could've stripped paint. "Gee, thanks. For what it's worth, I believe he's sincere. But I haven't decided one way or the other."

"Again, why not?" Gabi pushed.

"It's complicated, *hermanita*. He *is* my landlord

now." If I'd believed for a moment Hoyt would use that against me in the event we tried dating and it didn't work out, I'd never have signed the lease. But I still didn't quite know what to make of him or his interest.

"Right. Who everybody thinks you're already dating. Why wouldn't you want all the benefits of that being real?"

"Please stop," Rios begged. "I can't think about what any of that actually means."

Gabi stuck her tongue out at him.

Apparently desperate to let the subject drop, my brother folded his arms and pivoted to take in the kitchen. "Getting this place habitable is gonna take a lot of work."

"It's not like we don't have plenty of experience cleaning." I'd brought the supplies in my car to get started.

"There's also the fact that it's going to need to be furnished. You know Dad's not going to let you take anything out of the house."

"That's fine. I don't want to take anything except what's mine. My clothes, the stuff in our room, whatever. And if I need to move it out and leave a letter informing him, well, I intend to be gone before he gets it." Maybe that was the chicken shit way to handle it, but direct confrontation never went well with Hector Carrera. "I intend for all of us to be gone before he gets it." God knew, I didn't want either of my siblings to pay for what he'd perceive as my sins if they were still in the house.

Rios scooped a hand through the curling mop of his hair. "He's not going to take that well."

"He was never going to take it well. Can you think of a better way to handle it?"

After a moment's consideration, he shook his head. "Yeah, I got nothing."

"Look, I didn't do this just for myself. I know Gabi's headed off to school in a couple of months, and your plans haven't been firmed up yet, but there's room for all of us here."

Gabi bumped Rios on the shoulder. "Can you get over your overprotectiveness and look at the opportunity we have here? We can make our own home. A real one. No more tiptoeing around. No more having to abide by all his rules. Don't you want that?"

"Of course I want that."

I knew then that we had him. He could never say no to Gabi.

"Fine. The lease is signed. We might as well make the most of it."

"Yay!" She bounced up and threw her arms

around him, pressing a noisy kiss to his stubbled cheek. "Let's start talking about paint colors and who gets which room."

My sister's excitement fueled my own as I gave them the grand tour, such as it was. Room by room, we discussed the work that needed to be done. As I had said to Hoyt, the place needed a lot of TLC. There were probably bigger things that would need to be done in the long term. But he'd told me straight out that I could paint whatever I wanted. I'd never been able to choose a color for my room before. The idea of it filled me with a ridiculous level of excitement.

In the end, Gabi and I got the bedrooms on the top floor, and Rios was taking the bottom. I suspected he chose that one because he'd be closest to the door, should we have any unplanned visitors.

"Well, there's a hell of a lot of painting that needs to be done before we move in," he announced. "That'll give us time to get some air mattresses and other basics. At least you'll have a work crew."

I looked up from the notebook where I'd been making lists of projects. "Oh?"

"Ford and Jace get back on-island tomorrow. I'll round up both of them and Sawyer. With all six of us, we ought to be able to make short work of this."

"You don't have to do that. They're only just back." Certainly, the last thing any of his friends wanted to do was to be put to work.

Rios swung an arm around my shoulders. "Let us do something for you for once."

I leaned into him, soaking up the comfort of family solidarity. This would be a good move for all of us. He'd see.

My phone buzzed with a text, breaking the moment. Pulling it from my back pocket, I glanced at the screen and felt my stomach drop.

> Hoyt: We need to talk about something important regarding the house.

Heart tripping with anxiety, I stared at his message and felt my newfound sense of freedom wilt with uncertainty.

Had Hoyt changed his mind?

9

HOYT

Caroline: Fine.

I might not have been in a relationship in a while, but I was well aware that this concession was hard won.

I hadn't been trying to start a fight this morning. I'd just wanted to make it clear that I'd be paying for any paint or other materials she'd be using on the house. The hardware store had already set up my account, and I'd called to add her to it first thing, because I didn't want the burden of the cost of materials to fall on her.

You'd have thought I'd insulted her first born considering how she reacted. At least, that was my interpretation of her text responses. She'd tried to insist she could cover her own costs. I pointed out that anything she did was staying with the house I owned, so it only made sense that I pay for it. She'd finally relented. Grudgingly. I really hoped she didn't severely limit what she wanted to do just because I was footing the bill. While I wasn't a rich man, I could certainly afford a bunch of paint.

I wondered if this was going to torpedo my chances at our relationship becoming a real one. Once the subject of her tenancy came up, the question of real or fake dating had been dropped. I hadn't wanted to do anything to pressure her. Which meant I also hadn't kissed her or touched her again after that unguarded moment in the kitchen. Even so, the dinner itself had gone great. She liked my cooking—bonus—and we'd enjoyed each other's company. At least, I thought we had.

Maybe I'd be able to turn it into a more regular thing, given she'd be right next door. Granted, with both of her siblings. But still. I wanted to spend more time with her. Because I just... liked her as a person. Beyond the attraction. Once she loosened up a little from the wine and being out of the public eye, she was really smart and funny, with occasional irreverent remarks I hadn't expected. I wanted to see what else was under all those layers of caution.

And, okay, also under those layers of fabric. I'd spent half the night fighting the urge to trace those little spaghetti straps where they draped over her shoulders. Proof that I still had a pulse. I could still see them in my head, still imagine what it would've been like to nudge them down and follow the trail with my mouth—

"McNamara, see you in my office?"

I shook off my musings.

Right. I was on shift. There was work to do.

Shoving up from the table, I followed Chief Thompson into his office and shut the door. The room smelled of coffee and the barest hint of smoke that seemed to have soaked into the very walls of the firehouse. Papers were strewn across Thompson's desk, and I recognized photos from the open investigation.

As I took a seat, I nodded toward them. "So, what's the latest on the beach house fire?"

"It's almost certainly arson, but we don't know the who or the why."

I had to fight to remain casual. "Do you consider Caroline sufficiently cleared?"

Thompson studied me for a long moment. "By rights, I should exclude you entirely from this investigation due to lack of objectivity, because of your involvement with a person of interest."

I knew that. It was why he hadn't used me more than absolutely necessary in the immediate aftermath of the fire. Him allowing me to come along when he questioned Caroline had been a professional courtesy that had skated a few lines. I had considered telling him the truth about our relationship status or lack thereof, but I'd realized it didn't matter. Either way, I wasn't objective about her.

But Thompson had hesitated instead of saying an outright no.

"But?"

"But you have more investigative training and experience than the rest of the department. So, while I can't have you actively investigating, I want your insight."

I could live with that compromise. "Do you believe Caroline set that fire?"

"If I did, I'd hardly have you sitting in that chair. But no, apart from the fact that she'd get no financial gain, no insurance payout, and has no history of trouble with her employer, the timeline doesn't fit. She was already across island starting her shift at the tavern well before the fire began. And while you and I both know that there are ways to set up a delay, there was no evidence of that in the debris."

I relaxed a little. "Okay."

The chief kicked back in his chair. "The sister's alibi also checks out, as does the brother's."

"You asked about Rios? Why? Is there some connection there that we didn't originally know about?"

"No. Just covering our bases. I didn't actually think he had anything to do with it. But he's a favorite scapegoat on this island right now, and the chief of police will investigate him one way or the other because he's got a hard-on for him. Figures if he can't pin him for the Busby girl, he'll get him on something else."

I had nothing good to say about Bill Carson. He'd been chief of police for most of my life, and while I hadn't had any run-ins with him, I knew others who had. He wasn't what you could call a fair and impartial sort of man to begin with, and I'd spent a fair amount of time wondering whether his obsession with Rios was because he truly believed Caroline's brother capable of harming someone or because he was just a racist son of a bitch. I appreciated Thompson's doing due diligence ahead of time.

"That's true enough. So, where are we? Give me the overview."

"We have a case of probable arson—not a particularly sophisticated one—that left the kitchen of the beach house a total disaster, caused damage to the structural integrity of the second floor, and likely would have taken out the entire house had it not been caught so quickly by the Newmans."

I considered. "They arrived more or less when they'd told the rental company they'd be arriving, so either the person setting the fire wasn't aware of the schedule or wanted the blaze to be stopped before it could get fully involved. The latter doesn't really make sense unless the insurance was the point."

"I can see something else is circling around in your brain. Keep going."

"Is it a matter of convenience that the fuel used was readily available cleaning supplies, or was it meant to make it look like Caroline was the guilty party?"

"It's possible. To what end?"

"Somehow striking back at her instead of her brother?" I shook my head. "That feels far fetched. I might just be paranoid on her behalf. What if it wasn't a particular effort to frame Caroline? Maybe it was simply meant to look like an accident. The kind of thing that insurance would still cover. There were no trailers, no fuel scattered else- where. It literally looks as if someone set a tub of cleaning supplies on the stove and turned on the burner. Oh, whoops. My bad. That's terrible. Can I have a check now?"

"That's certainly a decent working theory. We'll need to get local PD to look into Jim Foster's personal and company finances. Certainly his insurance is going to want a ruling one way or the other before they're going to pay out. We've put in for the State Fire Marshal to come out, but we're way on down his list. We've done as much evidence collection as possible and passed that on to the lab. Again, that'll take time to come back. So we're in a holding pattern. This is largely going to be a waiting game."

"Often is. When was the last time you had arson on the island?"

"Aside from the usual contingent of kids playing with shit they aren't supposed to, about three years back, we had a fire at the marina office. Late night fire that took out the whole damned building, including some pretty valuable navigation equipment and historical records. It all ended up being because the marina manager couldn't keep it in his pants. His wife found out about the infidelity and went to confront him about it up at the office, which was, coincidentally, where he met his mistresses."

"Plural?"

"Yup. He wasn't there at the time, but she had a right hissy fit and started trashing the place. Broke a lamp that sparked on all the heaps of paperwork on the desk and one thing led to another... You know how that goes."

"I do, indeed."

"Anyway, she tried to get things under control but couldn't find the fire extinguisher and ended up fleeing the scene. By the time we got there, nothing could be done to save the building. In the course of the investigation, we started digging into the manager's world and found out about the split with the wife. Went to talk to her, and she ended up breaking down in the interview and admitting to the whole thing. It was a damned mess, even though the investigation itself wrapped pretty quickly."

"Sounds like. Don't know that we'll be eliciting a blanket confession like that on this one."

"Hope springs eternal. Gotta figure out who we can put some pressure on. Thanks for your thoughts. I'll pass them on to Chief Carson."

Recognizing the conversation was done, I shoved to my feet. "If I can be of any more help, just let me know."

"I will. And McNamara, about this thing you've got going on with Caroline Carrera."

I tensed. "What about her?"

"Just watch yourself. Make no mistake—I think she's a nice girl. But trouble sticks to that family like sandburs, and I don't want to see you get caught up in that."

"I can handle whatever trouble comes my way."

"I hope that's true, son."

The blare of the alarm cut off any further reply I might have made. I bolted from Thompson's office, heading straight for my locker. It was time to suit up and roll out.

10

CAROLINE

"Welcome home! Thank you for helping." I wrapped Ford in a hug and found myself enveloped by big, burly arms that hit me even higher than they had when he'd been home at Christmas. "My God, did you grow *again?*"

Ford laughed and scooped a hand through his mop of brown hair that was well past needing a cut. "Thank you. You're welcome. And yeah. I'm up to 6' 3" now."

"What are they feeding you down in Georgia?" He'd headed to UGA on a track and field scholarship, so I expected him to be in good shape, but this was getting ridiculous.

He patted his flat, muscled abs. "Anything I

want."

"You men and your ridiculous metabolisms," I groused. "Jace, bring it in."

The last of the Wayward Sons stepped in for a hug himself. "Good to see you, Caroline."

"Likewise." I pulled back to study him, noting the shadows in his eyes that hadn't been there last time he'd been home.

Something big on his mind.

He'd sort it out with the boys. And if he didn't, I could do a little sisterly poking. What was the point of having three extra unofficial brothers if I couldn't treat them all like family?

"So, you and Hoyt McNamara, huh?" Ford prompted.

I glared at Rios. "Seriously? You already told them?"

"Hey, I didn't tell them anything."

"Actually, I heard it from Mimi," Ford admitted. "She's delighted, by the way."

I'd always loved Delilah Washington. A free-spirited, hippie-type artist, she was an unexpected partner to Ford's biological mom, Florence Donoghue. But the two women had a bond like no couple I'd ever seen, and they'd been unofficial moms to the rest of us. Given we were all missing solid maternal figures in our lives, that had always been appreciated. But damn if the woman didn't adore her gossip.

Because they were all staring at me expectantly, I pinched the bridge of my nose. "Things with Hoyt are complicated." That had been my party line, and I was no closer to an actual decision on whether we were real or fake dating than I had been when the initial question was posed. After the whole sort of fight we'd had about him paying for any home improvement materials, I wasn't even sure if real was still on the table. I hadn't seen him during his two days off before he went back on duty.

"Well, yeah, dating your landlord could end up a sticky situation," Jace pointed out.

I narrowed my eyes. "The thought had occurred to me."

"Seems like he's being good to you," Sawyer put in. "That's the important thing. Well, and that he makes you happy. Does he?"

Whatever this thing with Hoyt was couldn't be summed up so simply as him making me happy. Particularly as we hadn't actually done any actual dating besides the one dinner at his place. The dinner where he'd taken the time to pick flowers, even though he wasn't even moved in yet. The one where he hadn't pushed for a decision on our status, even though that had been the original point.

"He's good to her," Gabi insisted. "He's stood up for her in front of jerks on several occasions."

My sister wasn't going to be satisfied until I actually said yes.

I waited for Rios to point out that we weren't even really dating at this point. But for once, my brother was quiet. And if he hadn't already spilled that detail to his friends, maybe he didn't plan to. At least, not until I'd made whatever decision I was going to make.

"That's good enough for me," Ford announced. "So you've got primer up in here. What about the rest of the place?"

"Gabi, Rios, and I were here until two this morning, knocking out the primer." A decision I knew I'd regret about halfway through work tonight. "I'm hoping we can get the first coat on everywhere else before I have to leave for my shift at the tavern."

Jace clapped his hands. "Then let's get to it."

"There's pizza in it for all of you when we break."

"Always a valid form of payment," Sawyer insisted.

I gave them the quick tour and divvied up assignments. We elected to knock out the downstairs first. I passed out the rollers and paint trays I'd picked up from the hardware store and reluctantly charged to Hoyt's account. I still didn't like this feeling that I wasn't fully paying my way, so I'd make up for it in doing a hell of a good job with the actual work.

One of the guys started a classic rock playlist on his phone, and we dove in. Conversation was easy and simple—a lot of the boys ragging on each other, catching up in the way of friends who were never truly apart, no matter where life took them.

"So, I broke up with Emily."

I glanced over at Ford, who was dutifully applying a coat of warm, buttery yellow to the living room wall. "Isn't this, like, the third time?"

"I thought it was the fourth," Sawyer remarked.

"No, no. Remember? There was that other time they broke up during sophomore year," Jace added. "Over the—what was it?—the thing with her roommate?"

To say that Ford and his college girlfriend had been on again off again for their entire college career was an understatement. I'd been hearing secondhand stories of their relationship since he came home for Christmas freshman year.

Ford's broad shoulders hunched up toward his ears, and he kept his attention on the wall. "Counting all the times either of us broke up with each other, it was five."

In my opinion, if breaking up was ever on the table, the correct answer was breaking up and staying that way. But I wasn't sure Ford was ready for that kind of tough love yet, so I held my tongue.

Rios had no such qualms about busting Ford's chops. "Are we taking bets on how long it takes you two to get back together?"

"No. I think we're really done this time." Ford refilled his roller. "I mean, the fact that we keep going off again is a sign, right? There's some underlying reason for that, and that's not a good basis for a long-term relationship."

Sawyer shot a fist into the air. "He can be taught!"

Ford scowled. "Man, don't be a dick."

Jace clapped him on the shoulder. "We're not being dicks. But seriously, I think this is a good thing. She's messed up your head enough. Maybe take some time on your own, figure out what you really want in a partner. Or more importantly, in life. Let the partner come later."

Look at these guys, making solid relationship suggestions.

Ford dropped his shoulders and nodded. "Yeah, I think that's a good idea."

I dipped my brush into the paint and continued cutting in at the edges. Bree was going to be really happy to hear this. Whether she had a thing for Ford or not, she'd always despised Emily. Maybe with her out of the way, Bree could finally figure out how she really felt. Would she be brave enough to take that leap this summer or let the opportunity pass her by?

Rios hauled his tray across the room and refilled it with paint. "So Ford is newly single. What's new with you, J?"

"Well, there's the fact that my parents have every expectation that I'm going to finish school next year and go directly to Ivy League law school. Do not pass 'Go.' Do not collect $200. Go directly to jail. It's the last thing I want to do. I'm trying to decide what to do about it."

"What would you want to do if your parents' opinions didn't come into play?" It was a question I wasn't sure Jace had ever considered.

"Hell, I don't know. I know I don't want to be a lawyer. I don't want to be a suit. The idea of corporate anything kills my soul. And anything else is going to cause a family war. I need to know that Willa's okay before I think about rocking the boat that much."

Beside me, Sawyer tensed. "That sounds like she's not okay. What's going on?"

"What's going on is that she is now eighteen and determined to get out from under our parents' thumbs. She's always resented that they took her off-island after..." Jace waved a hand, encompassing the whole messy situation.

The same night Gwen Busby had disappeared from a beach party, Willa had nearly drowned while trying to save a dog on the ocean side of the island. She'd gotten caught in a riptide. Sawyer had been the one to save her. The one to keep up the rescue breathing until paramedics could arrive. I didn't know any of the other details about what had happened after, only that her parents had moved off Hatterwick, and taken Willa with them against her protests. Jace and Willa's grandparents were still here, but none of the rest of the family had been back to visit besides Jace.

"So, what are her plans?" Gabi's voice was cautiously hopeful. She and Willa had been friends, but I knew that they'd fallen apart over the last couple of years. Privately, I thought that was more because of Willa's parents than Willa herself, for all the same reasons they hated Jace being friends with Rios.

"She's moving back to the island. Supposed to get here at the end of the week. She'll be looking for a job, so if anybody knows of anything, please let me know."

I perked up at that. "Well, it may not pay enough, but we just lost a server at the tavern and haven't replaced her yet. I feel certain I can talk Ed into taking her on."

"Oh, thanks. That would be awesome. I'll pass that along."

"Obviously, her first priority will be a job and a place to live," Rios said. "Think she'll stay with your grandparents?"

Jace shook his head. "No, she's very insistent that she be on her own. She doesn't want help from any of them." He lowered his voice. "Not that it's likely our parents would help her stay on-island anyway, given how they feel about the place."

I wondered what the Sutters would do or say with the return of their granddaughter. Except Ford and his moms, none of the rest of us had great family situations. There was a lot of strain and tension in the Hollingsworth household. I didn't know if their grandparents would welcome Willa or not.

Gabi cocked her head, considering. "Why is Willa so determined to do everything on her own?"

Jace's jaw went hard. "Let's just say that our parents aren't great people. And the things they've put her through the last couple of years..." He shook his head again. "Being away at school, I didn't realize how bad it was. And I don't think she's told me everything. It's good she's getting out on her own."

We all exchanged worried looks. Somehow, the lack of details made everything he didn't describe that much worse.

After a long minute, Gabi asked, "Is she going off to college in the fall?"

"Right now, she's taking some time. She wants to come home and see what she can manage. I'll help however I can." Jace's tone made it clear he didn't think it would be enough to make up for whatever she'd been through while he was off at school.

All of this was just proof that it didn't matter what social class you came from, you could always have shitty family. It was why we fought so hard to hang on to the one we'd made.

I laid a hand on his arm. "You know we'll all

look out for her, too, the way y'all have always looked out for me and Gabi."

"Appreciate that. She can definitely use some people she can trust."

Don't we all.

I thought again of Hoyt. Obviously, I trusted him on some level. He'd proved himself to be an honorable man. But did I trust he could handle whatever might come of us being legitimately involved? Did I trust him enough to take a risk with my heart? Because there was no question that if I made that choice, I'd catch feelings. That high school crush had only been the beginning, and he was so much more now than he'd been back then.

There was only one way to find out.

11

HOYT

I left the firehouse well after the end of my shift, having stuck around to assist with some training exercises with the volunteer fire-fighters who helped round out our small department. It had been a long few days. In my off-time between my last two shifts, I'd been pulled in to help my family diagnose and repair an engine problem on the cabin cruiser Drew had purchased with long-term plans to book fishing trips for tourists, so I'd barely spent any time at my own place before heading back to work, where we were slammed with several medical calls and a string of trash can fires at the same end of the island as the beach house that had burned. We'd been able to get out there and put out the flames before they'd jumped to the houses themselves, save for one, and that one had been caught by the renter on premises and put out with a garden hose. In all three cases, the origin had been a smoldering cigarette butt. If there'd been only one, we might have chalked it up to carelessness. But three set not more than an hour apart, at houses within the same mile stretch as the original arson? That was something else. Were they connected? I didn't know. If there'd been progress on the beach house fire investigation, Chief wasn't sharing. It was just as possible we were still in that holding pattern.

During all those days, I hadn't communicated with Caroline beyond a quick text to make sure she'd gotten everything she needed. Her answer had been one word—*Yep*—and nothing more. She hadn't been at the house during my brief stay at home. Working, probably. But the whole thing made me feel like our disagreement over who was paying for supplies had been a real fight that was fucking up a real relationship, and I wanted to fix it.

That would require finding her first. She hadn't mentioned when she was moving in. I wasn't sure if she intended to paint beforehand or was more eager to get out of her father's house. If I were a betting man, I'd have wagered on the latter, but I suspected that her getting her own place and taking her siblings with her was going to involve a more careful extraction than it would for normal people. Given her insistence on driving herself to our dinner, I sensed that my showing up at their house looking for her wouldn't go over well if her dad was around. I didn't want to cause her any more trouble than she already had, so I'd be patient. Meanwhile, I'd figure out what I could do to make up for the fact that I'd probably wounded her pride over the renovation supplies.

All intentions for planning flew out the window when I got home and spotted Caroline's car peeking out from behind some of the overgrown beach grass. Faint strains of music reached me from her side of the house as I stepped out of my truck. She was here.

My exhaustion fell away as I climbed the steps and made my way around to her door. I just... needed to see her. The closer I got, the better I could make out the music—something old school. Was that Dean Martin? My mom loved him. The windows were cracked, and I heard the faint sound of her singing along to "Mambo Italiano" in a rich alto. The sound of it made me grin. I liked the idea that she had music while she was working. At least, I assumed she was working, either on the house or on unpacking, since she was here instead of on shift at the tavern. It sounded like she was having fun.

Without giving myself time to overthink it, I knocked.

A moment later, the music turned down. Then the door swung open and there she stood in a slouchy t-shirt and cutoffs, her feet bare, her hair gathered up in another of those messy buns. She looked good enough to eat.

"Hi." *Brilliant, McNamara. She should throw herself into your arms immediately.*

Her lips curved into a smile that was a little bit shy around the edges, but seemed genuine. "Hey."

Maybe the whole text exchange hadn't been as much of a thing as I feared? We didn't know each other that well yet. Maybe I read a bunch of irritation into her tone that wasn't there.

"I saw your car and thought I'd come over to check in."

She rocked a little on those bare feet, drawing my attention to her toes. They were painted chili pepper red. For some reason, I found that tiny glimpse behind the curtain unaccountably sexy. I loved knowing that behind that usually reserved demeanor, she had sassy toes. Could toes be sassy?

"Um... do you want to come in?"

I yanked my focus back to her face to find her mouth pursed in amusement. Damn if that didn't just make me want to kiss her. "Yeah." I stepped inside. "How's the painting going?"

"It's finished." She waved a hand.

Finally dragging my attention away from her lips, I glanced around the room. Then I did a double take and straight up stared. The floors were still a scarred mess that needed refinishing, but all the walls had a fresh coat of paint in a pale, buttery yellow. The trim was a crisp, bright white. Even the ugly ass kitchen cabinets had been painted a deep turquoise that I wouldn't have thought would work with the yellow walls but still somehow did.

"Holy shit."

"I'm so sorry. I should have run paint colors by you before I went and did it." She caught her lush bottom lip between her teeth, her eyes turning worried.

"No, no. I'm not upset. It looks cheerful and happy. I'm just amazed at how much you managed to get done in the last few days. Are you secretly Wonder Woman?"

The distress melted away, and she laughed. "No. My brother's friends are back on-island for the summer, so between all of them and Gabi, I had a full painting crew. None of us have slept much, but everything is painted."

"Shit. Do y'all hire out?"

That laugh rolled out again, rich and easy. "Sadly, they'd charge you more than the beer and pizza they charged me."

I moved further into the room, examining their work. They hadn't half-assed it. "I think it would be worth it."

"If you really want, I can ask."

She'd used a big wooden wire spool with one side removed as a kitchen table. It, too, had been painted that deep turquoise. A quartet of wooden crates was tucked beneath it for stools. The jar of wildflowers in the center of the table made me smile as I thought back to our date the other night.

"This is great. Really clever—what's it called? —upcycling?"

"I'm gonna turn the other round into a coffee table, but I've still got to find something for legs." She stood with her hands shoved into her back pockets. "We're still working on picking up furniture. Starting with air mattresses on the floor for now, and shelves made out of cinder blocks and wood planks. It's not much, but it's a start. It'll do until the next payday when we go pick up the sofa Beachcomber Bargains is hanging onto for us and see what else we can come up with. Gabi's making it her life's mission to dumpster dive on the rich side of the island."

I met her gaze, and her golden cheeks deepened in color, as if the admission embarrassed her a little.

"Hey, they throw out some good stuff."

"They do. And it's fun to see what you can find and turn into something new."

It struck me then that she looked happy in a way I hadn't seen before. As if a weight had slid off her shoulders. If I'd had any doubts about offering this place to her, they died a swift death. Being able to take something off her plate was worth it. She'd nested so fast into having her own home, and I was fascinated to see what other little touches she added as things progressed.

"So is the move still in progress, or are you really here?"

"Officially here. This is the first night in the new place."

I realized I hadn't heard anyone else since I'd arrived. "Is Gabi not here to celebrate?"

"Oh no, she ran away to hang out with her friends. I think she was afraid I'd put her back to work."

I didn't want to do anything to dim that happiness, but I had to ask. "How did your dad take it?"

She shrugged. "Honestly, I don't know. I haven't told him directly. We moved our stuff out while he was at work today, and I left a note without my new address. I predict it's going to go over like a lead balloon."

Ah. Hence why her car was partly hidden.

"You worried?"

"Not any more than usual. Rios will be home later."

Hector was a controlling son of a bitch. In all likelihood, he was only just getting home to find out that all his children had defected today. Lead balloon was probably an understatement for how he'd react. She might not have told him where she was moving to, but it probably wouldn't take him too long to find out.

"How about I stick around in the meantime, just to make sure you're okay? You ought to be perfectly safe in your new place—" *Please, God, don't make a liar out of me.* "—but I don't like the idea of you being here by yourself, just in case." I braced myself for a turn in mood. For an accusation that I was overstepping. For annoyance that I was somehow raining on her parade.

Instead, a mix of relief and pleasure flickered

over her face. "Well, at least let me return the favor and feed you some dinner as a thank you."

"I will never say no to food. But I have one condition."

One dark brow winged up. "Which is?"

"You let me help. I don't sit around well."

"That's a deal. Wash up. I was just getting ready to start cooking."

I moved to the sink. "What's on the menu?"

"Pan seared whatever fish my brother caught this morning, with mango salsa and cilantro-lime rice." She paused, one hand on the open fridge door. "Wait, are you one of the soap people?"

"Soap people?"

"The ones who don't have the enzyme to taste cilantro properly. Bree's like that. She says it tastes like somebody dumped a bottle of dish soap into the food."

"So far as I know, I'm safe there." I eyed the ingredients she'd piled on the counter. Mango, red onion, jalapeno, red bell pepper, a lime, and a bunch of green stuff I presumed was cilantro. "Oh, you're hard-core making your own fresh salsa?"

"It's so much better that way."

"I approve. What can I do?"

"Salsa first, so we should get to chopping. You

take the bell pepper and onion. I'll do the mango and jalapeno."

She turned the music back up before dragging out a couple of plastic cutting mats and knives, and we got to work. Because the house's kitchen had been truly cut in half, there was minimal counter space. That meant we were shoulder to shoulder at the lone stretch of butcher-block-style formica that wasn't taken up by the sink. I was extra aware of her beside me as the music rolled into Sinatra's "The Way You Look Tonight."

"So you're a fan of The Rat Pack?"

"This is my happy cooking music playlist. Since I've got nobody to please but myself here tonight, I'm indulging."

My knife thunked down hard through the bell pepper as my brain took a very inappropriate detour about how I could please her. If I didn't get my head on what I was actually supposed to be doing, I'd lose a finger.

"I grew up on this music. My mom loves them."

"They're classics for a reason. No matter how much Rios and Gabi roll their eyes at me."

I carefully scraped out the seeds and ribs and began to dice. "Pretty sure it is a sibling's sworn duty to give us shit."

She neatly halved the mangos. "Do you and Drew rag on each other?"

"Absolutely. He's given me plenty of crap for buying this house. He thinks it'll be an albatross."

"Rude." Caroline lifted a hand to stroke the freshly painted cabinet. "She just needs some love."

"That's what I said. I'm not afraid of hard work. I think the payoff will be worth it in the end."

When she didn't answer, I glanced over to find her head bowed, her fingers flexing on the spoon she was using to scrape the scored mango flesh into a bowl. Abruptly, she muttered something I recognized as a curse in Spanish and dropped the spoon and fruit. Then her hand was fisting in my shirt, dragging me closer to close her mouth over mine.

Oh, thank God.

I dropped the knife onto the counter with a clatter and gripped her hips, hauling her closer. Her arms twined around my neck, and her lips opened beneath mine. There was nothing hesitant or innocent about this kiss. It was incendiary. Everywhere her curvy body pressed against mine set me aflame. It took all the control I had not to take over and back her against the nearest counter so I could plunder her mouth more thoroughly.

She'd started this. I wasn't going to push for more than she wanted to give, even if my dick was standing up to shout, "Hooray!"

I was dimly aware of "Somewhere Beyond the Sea" winding down when she eased back. Her eyes were blown so wide, the irises had all but disappeared. Her breasts rose and fell against my chest with each breath, and those beautiful lips were pink and swollen from mine.

I couldn't stop myself from asking the first thing to pop into my head. "Am I to take that to mean this dating thing is real?"

The corner of that gorgeous mouth quirked. "If you have to ask, I didn't do my job well enough."

I grinned, and this time I did back her against the counter, caging her in between my arms as I leaned in close. "Maybe we should try it again, just to be sure."

12

CAROLINE

"Do you think Ford's really serious about being done with Emily?"

Bree didn't look up at my question, but her shoulders hitched in a shrug that was anything but casual. "Who knows? He hasn't done more than mention it to me in passing."

I could've let it go. Maybe should have. But the lull between lunch and dinner service left me with far too much time to think, and I couldn't quite resist pressing, just a little. "Are you going to do something about that?"

Her gray gaze flicked up to mine. "About what?"

"The fact that he's finally single and home for longer than a weekend."

Was that a flare of panic in her eyes? She glanced down before I could be certain.

"Maybe he needs to be single for a while. To deal with whatever his shit is before he moves on with someone else."

"Fair enough." It would be truly crappy if Bree took a shot at something more with Ford, only to end up as his rebound. Still, he was showing some maturity on the relationship front that I hadn't seen before. I could've said something to Bree about that, but ultimately, I let it drop. She'd make a move when and if she was ready. If that was never—well—that was her right and her loss. Even if I thought she and Ford were perfect for each other.

"What about you?"

Her question pulled me out of my musings. "What about me?"

"You apparently finally took a shot with the hottie firefighter. Everybody's talking about you and Hoyt. How's that going?"

I thought about last night's dinner, and about that sexy as hell kiss in my kitchen. If there'd been any doubt that the attraction was mutual, he'd put it thoroughly to rest. "It's going well."

'Well.' Such a bland word for the reality.

I remembered Hoyt caging me in against the counter with that big, muscled body of his, and shivered. Hell, if there hadn't been the chance of one of my siblings getting home at any moment, things might've gone a whole lot more than well. And that was a degree of reckless that was entirely unlike me. But I liked having his mouth on me. I loved the feel of those work-roughened hands touching me, and I wanted more.

God, when was the last time I'd actually *wanted* to be touched? When was the last time I'd trusted someone enough to want that?

Basically never.

So if I'd tossed restlessly half the night, imagining what it would've been like to drag him up to my room and explore each other as thoroughly as possible—well, at least I had a room to myself now.

"Uh-oh." Bree's muttering pulled me out of my fantasy. "Creep ahoy."

I spotted Troy Lincoln settling in at a table in my section and groaned. He made no effort to hide the fact that he was watching me.

"I can cover him," Bree offered.

"I won't say no." I hadn't seen Troy since the showdown with Hoyt, and I wasn't eager to start.

Especially not with the obvious resentment written all over his face. At least he was sober this time of day. Probably.

Bree abandoned the ketchups she was marrying and wandered over to take his order. I pretended to focus on the menus I was wiping down, but I could feel his eyes on me in the way my skin crawled.

"Caroline?"

At the quiet voice, I snapped to attention to find Willa Hollingsworth standing by the bar. Except this wasn't the girl I remembered hanging out with Gabi. That girl had been soft and a little bit fragile, with big hazel eyes that shone with hope and a heart that wanted to take in every animal on the island. This young woman had a wary toughness in her expression that spoke of a lack of trust in the world. It was a position I knew well from personal experience, and my heart went out to her for whatever had happened to destroy her innocence. Was it the near drowning? Or what came after?

"Willa! Welcome back to Hatterwick." I moved around the bar to embrace her. "It's good to see you."

Her answering hug came after only a few moments' hesitation. "You, too."

"How was Beaufort?" I knew that was where her parents had relocated when they'd left the island.

"I wouldn't know."

I blinked at the blunt statement that clearly implied she hadn't been in Beaufort with her parents. Which begged the question: Where had she been?

A distinct tension hung so heavily around the girl, there might as well have been a neon sign shouting *I don't want to talk about it* above her head. So I let it go. There'd be time to dig deeper later if the opportunity arose.

"Jace said you were looking for a job."

She nodded. "Anything I can find."

"It so happens we had a server quit last week, so there's an opening. Interested?"

"Very."

"Have you ever waited tables before?"

"No." For a moment her head dipped, her caramel brown hair swinging forward to hide her face before she lifted it again. "Is that a problem?"

"So long as you're willing to learn, you can be trained."

Because it was procedure, I went through the formal interview questions, even though I fully intended to hire her. Such was the prerogative of living in a small town. Then I described the job itself and the available hours. "You in?"

"Absolutely. I'm really grateful for the opportunity."

"Okay. You can start tomorrow, after I adjust the shift schedule." I filed the whole thing under the win column, even though training always took a bit of extra time and effort.

"Thank you!"

"Now, let's talk about—"

"Caroline Sofia Carrera!"

The furious shout had my shoulders hunching up to my ears, even before I whirled to see my father barging into the tavern. In less than a second, I registered the clenched fists, narrowed eyes, and muscle fluttering in his stubble-shadowed jaw. His cheeks were flushed nearly purple with rage as he stalked across the room.

Panic fluttered like a live thing in my throat, but I automatically slid in front of Willa. Not that he had eyes for anyone but me. "Dad."

"You ungrateful *puta*. How *dare* you? After everything I've done for you. Don't even bother to deny it. I know you were the one behind the others."

Every eye in the place was on us, but I didn't

dare take my focus off my father. "I can see you're upset—"

"Upset? *Upset?*" His voice rose loud enough to rattle the glassware. Then it dropped dangerously low. "You *left*. Without a word. Just like she did."

He meant my mother. I'd known this was a possibility when I elected to leave a note. At the time, it had seemed better than a direct confrontation. Now, I wasn't so sure.

Though I struggled to stay calm, my voice shook. "You would have tried to stop me."

"Damned straight. You have no right to—"

As emboldened as I was mortified by having witnesses, I let my own temper off its leash, just a little. "No right to a life of my own? That's where you're wrong, old man. I have every right. All three of us are legal adults. You have no hold over any of us anymore, and we choose to live on our own. There's nothing you can do about it."

He took a hard step closer, and everything in me wanted to recoil, to hide from the blow I was certain was coming. But he had enough control not to let loose that much in public. No, he saved the punches and slaps for private. With plenty of threats about what would happen if we didn't hide the resulting injuries. And they'd come much fewer and farther between since Rios got big enough to fight him. But I could see the promise of retribution in his eyes.

I dimly registered the sound of fast footsteps. Then multiple bodies were sliding between me and my father.

"I'm gonna need you to step back."

Hoyt. I almost sagged in relief. Did I broadcast some kind of alert every time I panicked that he could read as easily as the Bat Signal?

He'd brought friends this time. At least three other guys in navy SFFD T-shirts stood shoulder to shoulder, forming a human wall.

"This is none of your concern."

"As you're up in Caroline's grill, I'd say it is."

"Who the hell are you?"

"Her boyfriend. The one who's not going to hesitate to step between you and her."

I closed my eyes. Dad had probably already heard. Maybe. But somehow I felt it would be worse that he hear it from Hoyt directly.

"Now, do we have a problem, Mr. Carrera?"

For a long, tense moment, nobody spoke.

"No. No problem. Just a disagreement with my daughter." I couldn't see my father over all the shoulders, but I could hear him reining in the temper in the face of a greater implied threat.

"Maybe circle back to it later, when you're calmer," Hoyt suggested in an even tone. "And not in her place of work."

For a long humming beat, I waited, expecting my father to tell Hoyt exactly where he could shove that idea. Instead, he cleared his throat. "You're probably right. Apologies." The last word came out flat and entirely insincere.

He turned on heel and left without another word.

Then arms were sliding around me as Hoyt pulled me in, wrapping me up in his bigger body. "Hey, you okay?"

My throat went thick, because no, I definitely wasn't okay. I was shaking. This whole nightmare scenario had combined two things I hated: dealing with my father at all and being a public spectacle. I'd spent so much time being a public spectacle.

Hoyt stroked a hand down my back. He felt warm and solid, and I wanted so desperately to lean on him because I hadn't had anyone to do that with basically ever. It wasn't the same with my siblings. Rios did his best to take off whatever pressure he could, but there was no escaping the weight of being the oldest, of watching out for both my younger siblings in a volatile household. Of being the one who looked like Mama.

"What are you even doing here?"

"We were doing a training exercise. Bree texted to say there was trouble, so we came down."

I'd never been so glad that the firehouse was only two blocks down the street or that Hatterwick was the epitome of a small town. Someone had let him know, and he'd come for me. Did he have any idea how appealing that was? The fact that he was continually willing to step up for me made it feel like maybe this was the start of something real between us. Because it did, I let myself burrow in, holding on to him as an anchor in the storm that was my life.

"Saint Hoyt the Savior, coming down for your hero fix for the day."

Hoyt's body went stiff at Troy's mocking tone. "I don't recall asking for your opinion, Lincoln. I believe I made my position clear the last time I saw you. Stay the hell away from Caroline."

"I'm not doing a damned thing to her. Just came in for a late lunch. It's not like there are that many options."

"Maybe consider embracing the concept of brown bagging it."

"Whatever. I'm sick of your shit, McNamara."

"Likewise."

Not wanting the situation to escalate, I squeezed Hoyt's waist. "It's fine. He's not causing trouble."

"See?" Troy waved expansively. "Just enjoying this fine establishment."

Right. Because we all believed that.

Hoyt made a low, growling noise.

A radio crackled, and one of the other firefighters spoke. "L-T, we've gotta jet."

I felt him shift into work mode, his attention splitting toward the job. Hoyt stroked a thumb along my cheek. "I have to go."

Chances were, whatever he was rushing off to deal with was dangerous. That was the nature of his job. It was something I'd have to come to terms with if this thing between us was going to work.

"Be careful, okay?"

"Always." Brushing a fast kiss to my lips, he bolted for the door.

I prayed he'd be safe.

Feeling steadier than I had any right to be after everything that had happened, I turned back to the handful of gawkers. "Show's over. Go back to your meals."

Willa stood frozen where I'd left her by the bar.

Determined to get back to some semblance of normal, I pasted on a smile. "Sorry about that. Now, where were we?"

13

HOYT

Buying a house on the east side of the island was a risk. I'd take the brunt of any hurricanes that blew in. But this house had weathered those for decades and was still standing, so I'd considered it worth the gamble for everything I'd be gaining. As I sat on the second-floor porch in my newly assembled Adirondack chair, watching the sun slowly crest the horizon with Caroline curled up in my lap, I knew I'd been absolutely right.

"This is part of why I bought the house. I wanted to be able to sit here and watch the sunrise just like this."

She turned her head to look at me, her fingers twining in the hair at my nape. "Just like this?"

I tightened my arms around her. "I didn't have you in mind when I picked it out, but I'd say this is icing on a pretty awesome dream."

The corners of her mouth kicked up. "I don't hate it."

"I'd say I was sorry there's only one chair, but I'd be lying."

With a soft laugh, she nuzzled my cheek, then settled her head against my shoulder to keep watching the show Mother Nature was putting on across the water. The thin edge of light slowly lifted out of the ocean, brightening the burnt orange sky and bouncing off the thin scrim of clouds.

The only thing that could've made this better would've been if Caroline had spent the night in my bed. Still, it had been a great couple of days. An unexpectedly quiet couple of days that we'd spent more or less joined at the hip while she wasn't working. I'd finally done some work on my side of the duplex, taking a page out of her playbook and painting, just to have the sense that I'd made progress. Since I hadn't had a team of six to help me, I'd only gotten the downstairs primed, but it was still nice to see that blank canvas. The to-do list had been revised since I wouldn't be knocking down walls anytime soon.

That actually made the projects feel a little more manageable.

But my forty-eight hours were just about up, and I'd be going back on duty soon. I worried about leaving Caroline alone. There'd been no further sign of Hector. He hadn't approached Gabi or Rios. But that didn't mean he wouldn't the moment any of them were alone. Well, probably not Rios. But the girls?

I tipped my head to Caroline's. "I wish I didn't have to go to work."

"Mmm. A lazy Saturday would certainly be lovely. But even if you didn't have to go to work, I do. Marisol Gutiérrez hired me to help her set up her stall for the farmer's market."

"Oh yeah? Does she pay well?"

"Minimum wage. But she sets aside some of those gorgeous artisanal breads and pastries, too, so I call it a win."

"That certainly seems like a side-gig worth keeping."

Threading my fingers into the silky hair that had quickly become my obsession, I drew her mouth to mine for a soft, lingering kiss that tasted of the pre-dawn coffee we'd shared. She melted into me, a willing surrender that gave me all kinds of ideas we absolutely didn't have time for. On a groan, I pulled back. "I guess that will have to hold me."

"Guess it will." She darted back in for another quick kiss, then slid off my lap. "I've gotta get going. Be safe."

"Always."

"I'll see you tomorrow."

She started to pull away, but I used the hand I still held to tug her back against me for one more full body kiss that left her mouth swollen and my dick more than a little hopeful. "Don't forget me."

"Guh." At her blissed-out expression, I laughed and finally released her. She blinked and shook her head as if to clear it. "I think you need a license for that mouth."

Delighted, I waved her on her way. "I'm sure we can discuss that when I'm off-shift again. Go on. I'll text you later."

"Uh-huh."

When she still didn't move, I gently gripped her shoulders and turned her back toward the door to her room.

"Right. Later."

I was still on the upper gallery a couple minutes later when I heard the downstairs doors close and her car crank up. For a few more minutes, I debated with myself, then sent a text that very well might get me in trouble with Caroline later. If she found out.

No reply had come in by the time I headed into the firehouse a half hour later. The whole place smelled of bacon and coffee. I found everybody gathered family-style around the table inhaling biscuits and eggs along with that bacon. They had that amped up, post fire excitement going.

I poured myself another cup of coffee. "I gather it wasn't a quiet night?"

Jamal reached for another biscuit. "Our firebug seems to have struck again."

I braced myself. "Where?"

"You know that old beachcomber's shack on the south side? The one near Pelican's Rest?"

"The one the kids used to use as a lover's lane?"

"Still do. Or did. Won't be able to anymore," Smokey added. "Burned to the ground.

"Shit. Was anybody hurt?"

"Nobody was there," Jamal said. "And while we were dealing with *that*, somebody called in an unattended bonfire about two miles down the beach. We were damned lucky the wind was on our side last night. That one could've easily spread to all the marsh grass."

On autopilot, I loaded my plate. "Whoever it is, they're escalating."

"They're having a grand ol' time jerking us around is what they're doing," Tank muttered.

"How long until they set a fire to something actually occupied?" Pete asked.

"The question is whether these fires are connected to the beach house fire." I tapped my fingers against the side of my mug. "All the others have been easy access. Convenient outside garbage cans. Vacant property. That sort of thing. The house would've required either a key or breaking in. Who has the photos from the scene?"

Biscuit in hand, Jamal rose and went to retrieve them. "What are you looking for?"

I flipped through the images until I found the one I wanted. "Here. Back door. See those scratch marks around the lock? That wasn't from our breach. This door was jimmied."

Flash bit into a piece of bacon. "So what is this? Some kid bored with the summer? Since it's mostly been around the areas of rentals, could it be somebody who came in for vacation?"

"Gotta be somebody who's here for a while. How many folks stay here for two weeks or more?" Smokey asked.

"Could be somebody who has a beef with the tourist industry expansion," I mused.

We continued to discuss theories until Blaze stuck his head in the room. "Hey L-T, you got company."

I glanced beyond him to see Rios in the doorway.

So he'd decided to come in person instead of answering by text.

I was aware of everyone's gaze on me as I rose to meet him. "C'mon." I led him to the conference room where we conducted trainings. At this hour, it was empty. Perfect for a private conversation. "Thanks for coming."

Rios adopted a faux casual stance, resting one hip on the table. "What's up?"

"I'm worried about your dad. More specifically, the possibility that he'll target Caroline or Gabi when one of us isn't around. I figured you were the person to discuss things with to figure out what to do about it."

"What are you suggesting?"

"Well, in all honesty, even though I know your sister would happily skin me for the saying so, I'd like to put them both under some kind of protective detail."

Rios folded his arms and studied me. "What exactly are your intentions toward my sister?"

There were a lot of things I could've said, but I didn't have a good read on Rios and how he'd respond to any of them. As a rule, I preferred honesty wherever possible. "I intend to protect her. I care about her, and I don't want to see anything happen to her. Or to Gabi or you, for that matter."

The other man's brows drew together in skepticism. "Why do you give a shit about our family?"

"Look, I think you've all had a shit time of it. You, especially. Caroline matters to me, and I want to see her safe when I can't be there to make sure of it. I know it's not practical to expect anybody to be with her twenty-four-seven—not that she'd be okay with that if it was. But I think you can agree that your father represents a threat. Did she tell you about him confronting her at work the other night?"

A muscle jerked in his jaw. "No. But that doesn't surprise me in the least."

I filled him in.

Rios loosed a string of curses in Spanish. "Jury's still out on you, McNamara, but I agree with you on this. Sawyer and I have already been trading off as much as we can with our jobs, but I can lean on Jace and Ford a bit more. They haven't picked up jobs yet this summer. And I'll be having a conversation with both my sisters about keeping me informed if the asshole shows up."

"That'll be a start."

Someone outside shouted a split second before the alarm blared.

I opened the door to see Blaze racing toward a hose.

"Your fucking truck is on fire!"

"What?" I bolted outside, sprinting for the employee lot out back.

Sure enough, my pickup had flames shooting up from beneath the hood and inside the cab.

All around me, my crew leapt into action, quickly dousing the fire before it could spread. But my truck was toast.

"No way was that accidental," Jamal muttered.

Apparently, the chief had come in while I'd been talking to Rios. He arched his brows. "Who all have you pissed off lately?"

I thought about all the confrontations I'd had on Caroline's behalf in the past few weeks. "Quite a few people, as it happens."

14

CAROLINE

What a difference a day made.

This time yesterday, I'd been on top of the world. Or as close to it as I dared to reach. I'd been cuddled up in this chair with a thoughtful, sexy man who miraculously wanted *me*, and I'd thought that maybe, finally, something in life was going my way. That I'd finally earned something good.

That was over now. Or would be as soon as Hoyt got home.

I thought of the text he'd sent midmorning, an hour or two after the news of his truck being torched had spread across the island like—well—wildfire.

Hoyt: **I want to see you when I get off shift.**

If I'd needed any confirmation that this whole mess was my fault, that was it.

I'd considered heading straight to the firehouse to talk to him. But in the wake of the fire, he'd be working, doing investigative stuff and talking to the police. When he dumped me, I preferred that be here at home instead of in front of other people. I'd had enough of being a spectacle.

Of course, everyone was talking about it during my shift at the tavern. Someone had been ballsy enough to set his truck on fire *in the firehouse parking lot.* Speculation was running rampant about who it had been, and more than one pair of eyes fell on me. It had gotten so bad that an hour into my shift, Ed had taken pity and sent me to the back to work on inventory. Not something we usually did during service, but I was grateful for the reprieve.

Rios and Gabi had done their best to distract me once I'd gotten home. Neither of them brought up the obvious question: Would Hoyt ask us to move out?

But, damn, I'd thought about it all night as I'd tossed and turned, before finally giving up on sleep a couple of hours before dawn. We'd put so much work into painting this place, and I'd poured so much heart and effort into making it a home for all of us. Sure, it wasn't much—yet—but it was the first thing that had been ours in... ever. Now we'd have to leave because Hoyt wasn't ever going to want to see me again.

I'd warned him that getting involved with me would make him enemies. He'd blown that off, said it was no big deal.

But even he couldn't dispute that this was a big freaking deal. This wasn't just some verbal altercation. His truck had been destroyed. Maybe not blown up, but I'd been one of the gawkers to drive by. I'd seen the charred husk of the aftermath, had smelled the toxic stink of burnt rubber, melted plastic, and scorched metal, even from inside my car. There'd be no salvaging the vehicle.

I wasn't due at work until the lunch shift, and there were no cleaning jobs on my calendar this morning. I ought to try to snatch a few more hours of sleep, but I knew I wouldn't settle until this thing with Hoyt was finished. So I sat on the second floor porch, curled up in his chair, waiting and grieving what might have been.

I was still up there when someone pulled into the drive. I recognized Pete Novak behind the wheel. Hoyt slid out of the passenger side of the SUV and waved him off. Even from here, exhaustion was clear in every line of his body. He lifted his head, spotting me.

"Stay put. I'm coming up."

Just as well. My siblings were still asleep. It was better if we got this over with now, so I'd have time to figure out what to tell them in terms of what came next.

A few minutes later, he stepped out of his bedroom and waved me out of his chair. My heart sank as I rose because it felt like him waving me out of his life. I'd known this was coming, but God, it hurt. After all the time and effort I'd put into depending only on myself, how had I come to want him, to depend on him, this quickly?

Hoyt sank into the chair, his hand snaking out to grab mine and tug. Off-balance, I stumbled, falling straight into his lap. His arms wrapped around me, and his face buried in the messy knot of my hair. He sighed, a huge exhale that shifted us both.

"Ah, that's better. It's been a really shitty twenty-four hours."

What the hell was happening?

"I heard." Struggling to find my mental footing again, I launched into the apology I'd been planning since yesterday. "Hoyt, I'm so sorry. I knew you'd get blowback from being involved with me. And I just wanted to say that I get it. I understand."

He lifted his head. "You understand what?"

"Why we have to call this off."

There. I'd said it first. Look at me being all brave.

His brows drew together, his mouth tipping down into a frown. "What are you talking about?"

"Your truck was torched. It was my fault."

For a long moment, he just stared at me. "Unless you've suddenly developed powers of teleportation, you didn't light the match, so how is it your fault?"

"This whole thing has to be because you're involved with me. Because you stood up for me. Somebody's striking back at you." I loosed a bitter laugh. "Jesus, it's not even a short list. Why wouldn't you want to distance yourself?"

That frown dug even deeper. "Do you want me to distance myself?"

"Of course not!"

His face relaxed. "Okay, then."

"What I want isn't the point. You—"

Gently, he pressed a finger to my lips. "Hush for a minute and let me tell you about my day."

I subsided and listened as he told me what he could about the investigation. "It wasn't a sophisticated attempt. A couple of rags soaked in gasoline. One tossed through the windows I'd left cracked, one shoved into the engine compartment from beneath the truck. Whoever did it was in and out fast. There's footage from the bank ATM across the street of an adult male suspect entering the parking lot with a plastic shopping bag in hand. No face or distinguishing features visible. He wore a hat and sunglasses and seemed to know where the camera was. But we had a timestamp, so the police spent the day following up with several folks I've pissed off since I got back on-island. Among them, Troy Lincoln, your dad, Chet Banks, and Marcus Hoffman. Your dad and Marcus had alibis. Both at work. Neither Troy nor Chet can account for their whereabouts during the window in question, so the police are getting warrants to search their residences and vehicles."

I soaked that in. "Do you think either of them did it?"

"Hard to say. Proving who committed arson isn't always easy. A lot of the evidence is destroyed both by the fire and the suppression efforts. If there's no metaphorical smoking gun or, in this case, handy gas can with fingerprints available, it's tough to tie the crime to a particular suspect. But they're both on the police's radar."

"That's it?"

"Well, it is for me. Even if I were fully qualified to investigate, it'd be a conflict of interest. But if I had to guess, I'd say Troy is more likely than Chet. He's made retaliatory moves toward others in the past. Admittedly, not this extreme. But he is really pissed that I seem to have stolen what he believes is his." Hoyt's arms tightened around me in emphasis. "I'm not going to let any of this scare me off. First, because that would let an asshole win, and that's not gonna happen. And second, and much more important, because you matter to me. I meant what I said to him that night. I know a good thing when I see it, and I have no intention of giving you up. Not unless you want out."

This was exactly what I'd wanted to hear and hadn't dared let myself imagine. He still wanted this. He still wanted *me*.

My throat had gone thick with emotion, so I just shook my head. I didn't want out. But I still worried about how our involvement could impact him. Cuddling closer, I pressed a hand to his chest, feeling the steady, reassuring thump of his heart.

"What if this isn't the last time? What if this isn't the last thing?"

"We'll be on closer guard. The police are going to have Troy and Chet under a damned microscope, so I don't think either of them will be able to pull off anything. As far as I'm concerned, we continue business as usual. Morning coffee cuddles and cooking dinners together and dating like normal people."

"Just like that?"

"Just exactly like that."

Beneath my palm, his pulse didn't change. He truly was that laid back and relaxed about all of this. I realized a big part of what I found appealing about Hoyt was how solid and unshakeable he truly was.

One big, broad palm stroked my arm. "In the name of doing all that dating like normal people, I want you to come to dinner at my parents' place. Meet everybody properly."

The entire idea of facing down the rest of the McNamara clan absolutely terrified me. "I don't know about that. It seems like kind of a big deal."

"You're a big deal."

Well, didn't that make my heart go all fluttery? "Hoyt, meeting the parents is a serious thing."

"I'm serious about you."

Flummoxed, I could only stare at him. "But isn't this kind of fast?"

He shrugged. "I don't know that there's a specific timetable on such things. Do I need to slow down? Give you a chance to catch up?"

That was the thing that scared me most. I didn't need time to catch up because I was right there with him. "No."

"Then come to dinner."

It was the last thing I wanted to do. I didn't expect the meeting to go well. His parents couldn't be thrilled with the idea of him being with me. But he'd done so much for me. Going to this dinner and meeting his family seemed like the least I could do.

"Okay."

"We'll get it scheduled for our next mutual night off. Now—" He tightened his hold, cuddling me closer. "Give me some sugar to sweeten up this last crappy day."

Settled at last, I framed his face between my palms and pressed my lips to his. We both sighed into the kiss, melting into each other as we took comfort in this little piece of intimacy.

"Hey, Caroline, what do we have for breakfast? Rios is—Oh!" Gabi's voice cut off on a delighted little laugh. "Sorry about that. We'll get breakfast ourselves. Carry on."

As her footsteps retreated, we broke apart with mutual frustrated groans.

Hoyt pressed his face against my throat. "Maybe we should relocate inside. You could come and have a nap with me. I was up most of the night, and I'm beat."

A nap sounded good. Being wrapped up in his arms sounded even better. Dangerous, maybe. But I'd been thinking about crossing that line with him almost from the beginning. I wanted him. He wanted me. That was easy math.

I debated with myself as he led me into his room and over to the actual bed with a grown-up mattress and tugged me down onto it. When he hauled me into him as little spoon, wrapping me up tight, I decided now wasn't the right moment. I wasn't quite ready for anything more than this.

But as I slid toward sleep with the soft warmth of his breath stirring against my nape, I knew it had to be soon.

15

HOYT

"You ready?"

For just a moment, Caroline squeezed her eyes shut, her face a resolute mask. It was a stark contrast to the rest of her. The front half of her hair was pulled back from her face to reveal little silver hoops in her ears. She'd chosen a blue dress, but this one was more sedate than the sundress she'd worn for our first date, with a flowy skirt that hit past her knees, short little sleeves that just cupped her shoulders, and a straight neckline. Her open-toed sandals revealed a pretty shell-pink polish on her toes. I could see she'd added the same to her fingers.

"You look beautiful. But why do I feel you dressed like we're going to a church picnic?"

Insult whipped a little color into her cheeks. "I'm meeting *your parents*. I want to make a good impression."

I stepped in to skim my hands down her arms. "And you will. Relax, it's just dinner."

"'Just dinner,' he says." She picked up her purse and a small paper gift bag, and muttered something in Spanish that, judging by her tone, probably wasn't complimentary. "Let's go."

I laced my fingers with hers and lifted her hand so I could press a kiss to the back of it. "It'll be fine. They're going to love you."

"I really hope your faith isn't misplaced."

Did she mean my faith in her or my family? Either way, I was vaguely insulted. But as she was one step away from crawling out of her skin with nerves, I let it go. It had taken nearly a week and a half to coordinate schedules, and in all that time, Caroline had built this whole dinner up into some monumental thing. On top of which, I knew a lot of people had treated her and her family poorly. At this point, nothing but getting it over with was going to put her at ease.

We headed out to the loaner car I'd been using since the fire. Though the case was straightforward, it would still be a few weeks before insurance approved my claim and sent a check to cover the loss of my truck. In the meantime, Stan Jenkins, one of my dad's fishing buddies, had offered his antique 1980s Chevy pickup. It was a project vehicle Stan had been talking about restoring since I was old enough to peer into an engine compartment, and in all that time, he hadn't gotten much further than replacing the motor. But it was getting me from place to place, so I was hardly going to complain.

As I drove the short distance toward my parents' place in Sutter's Ferry, Caroline gripped the sea turtle pendant on her necklace like a lifeline, dragging it back and forth on the chain. Reaching across the bench seat, I found her hand with mine and linked our fingers again. She didn't look at me, but she held on tight, as if she'd be swept out to sea at any moment.

Her grip didn't relax as we pulled into the driveway of the house where I'd grown up. It was a quintessential coastal cottage, clad in weathered shingles that had taken on a soft, silvery-gray patina, and a cedar shake roof my mother loved for its rustic charm and my father cursed for being a pain in the ass. I had to side with Mom on that one. White trim around the windows offered a crisp, clean contrast, and the bright blue front door added a splash of color and whimsy that reminded me of Caroline and her kitchen cabinets.

I tugged her up the steps to the porch, past the rocking chairs and hanging planters with their profusion of red petunias, and went straight inside. "Hey! We're here!"

Mom popped out of the kitchen, her silver-streaked blonde hair tossed up in a ponytail, a checkered dish towel tossed over one shoulder. "Welcome!"

Beaming, she hurried across the room and embraced me like it had been a year instead of three days since she'd laid eyes on me. Then she turned to Caroline. "It is so nice to officially meet you, Caroline. I'm Ibbie." She waved a hand toward the open back door, where Dad was stepping inside. "And that's my husband, Frank."

"It's a pleasure to meet you, Mrs. McNamara. Mr. McNamara."

Mom waved that away. "Oh, now. Mrs. McNamara is my mother-in-law. Please, call me Ibbie."

Caroline shot me a look of vague panic before squaring her shoulders and offering the bag. "I brought you a little hostess gift."

"Ooo, presents. I love presents." Mom took the bag and dipped a hand inside. It was a pint jar of something golden.

"It's local honey from Golden Dunes Honey Company. And I added in a dozen or so of my favorite recipes, in case you needed ideas for how to use it."

As Mom reached back into the bag again, Dad offered a none-too-subtle thumbs up.

Mom drew out a neat stack of index cards tied with purple ribbon. "Oh, how thoughtful! I love it. Thank you." She wrapped an arm around Caroline's shoulders in a friendly squeeze that stunned Caroline so much, for a moment I thought she might cry.

Shit. I hated she wasn't used to casual affection or people being nice to her.

Before I could decide if and how I could rescue her, a timer went off. Dad waved a spatula. "That'll be the chicken. Y'all have good timing."

"Is there anything I can do to help?" Caroline asked.

"Everybody come grab a platter," Mom ordered. "Drew! Come make yourself useful, son!"

My brother materialized from somewhere, and we all headed for the kitchen, grabbing plates and bowls of food and hauling them out back.

Caroline stopped on a gasp two steps out the door. "Oh! This is wonderful."

Dad grinned from ear-to-ear. "It is, isn't it? Our own little slice of paradise."

Inside the fenced yard, my parents had planted an oasis of a garden that they'd nurtured over nearly three decades. It surrounded a wide patio that was shaded by one of the ancient live oaks that were sought after on the island. Beneath it, we'd built a long picnic table for the parties they liked to host. Tiki torches with citronella were already lit around the perimeter.

Mom brought up the rear and herded us all toward the table. Dad pulled the chicken off the grill, and we took our seats.

Drew dug out a big spoonful of potato salad. "So, what's the word on the investigation?"

"Drew!" Dad hissed.

"What? I just want the update. Especially since everybody's talking about those other fires."

Because I could feel Caroline going ramrod straight beside me, I reached over to lay a hand on her leg beneath the table. "It's still ongoing. They've narrowed it down to a couple of likely suspects, but conclusive evidence hasn't been tied to either of them. As for the other fires, they aren't believed to be connected to my truck."

There'd been a few mailbox fires and some additional old sheds, all further afield than the original fires. Our perpetrator was getting bolder, probably enjoying seeing the department dance. But I sure as shit didn't want to talk about work, even if I had been able to comment on an ongoing investigation.

"Shitty situation all around," Drew continued. "Do they know what the motive is?"

Beneath my palm, her thigh began to tremble with tension.

"Well, it happens that I've pissed a few people off since I came home." I kept my tone level as I attempted to glare my brother into submission.

"Son, hush. I need to say something." Mom fixed a level gaze on Caroline. "The entire legal system of our country was founded on the idea that anyone accused of a crime is innocent until proven guilty. They haven't proved your brother guilty of anything. So until or unless they do, as far as we're concerned, he's a victim of circumstance, and so are you. We do not in any way, shape, or form think you have anything to do with what's happened."

Mortified that she'd shone a spotlight on the elephant in the metaphorical room, I could only mutter, "Mom!"

"It's better to clear the air. Now, hopefully, Caroline will be able to relax a little better."

Beside me, Caroline took a careful sip of her tea. "I appreciate your perspective and that y'all are being so open-minded and welcoming me into your home." She paused before shifting her gaze up toward the tree. "Have you ever considered adding an outdoor chandelier? Something with candles would really add to the ambiance you've got going out here."

Then they were off talking about upcycling projects. My mom was in heaven. They both drew me into talking about the house and my plans for it. Mom still hadn't been by to see the place by my own refusal, but as she and Caroline continued to make suggestions, I knew I wouldn't be able to hold her off much longer. By the end of the meal, Mom had enough fodder for Dad's Honey-Do list that he'd be busy until the end of the decade, and I had a whole new level of enthusiasm for the home improvement projects I'd largely put off to spend time with Caroline. Best of all, my girl was smiling, and that made me feel like I'd won the lottery.

Mom rose from the table. "Hoyt, come help me bring out dessert. I made banana pudding."

"You are a goddess among women."

"Of course I am."

I followed her inside, prepared to have my hands laden with bowls.

She opened the fridge and pulled out the dish. "I really like her. The two of you seem great together."

I smiled. "Yeah, we are."

Mom patted my cheek. "You're a good boy, Hoyt."

When dessert was finished and the table cleared, Mom declared Drew was on dish duty and sent us on our way with neatly packaged leftovers and maternal hugs for us both. Caroline actually lingered a moment, squeezing back and thanking her for the invite.

"You'll come back," Mom announced.

"I will. Thanks."

The tone of the ride back was vastly different. I could see the faint curve of her mouth as she rode, clutching our containers of leftovers in her lap.

"My family really liked you."

She glanced over, smiling bigger. "I really liked them. It's a novel concept to spend time with a family like yours. They're really great. I hope you know that."

"Yeah, I do." And maybe that was something I hadn't always actively thought about. But I was thinking about it now. "I try not to take it for granted."

"That's good. We never had anybody *to* take for

granted. Our dad is... well, you've heard the rumors. And Mom. She left all of us with him without a backward glance so many years ago."

The idea of it broke my heart for all of them. I couldn't imagine a mother leaving her children with a known abuser. It was hard not to judge Caroline's absentee mom for that.

Catching the tightening around Caroline's mouth, I took her hand again and squeezed. "It's her loss. You're all great, despite your circumstances. And I feel pretty sure that the credit for your siblings goes to you."

The tension in her expression eased. "Someone had to step up. Rios and I both did, in different ways. Right now, we're just glad Gabi is getting the chance to do what we couldn't. Go off to school, have a new start away from all the baggage here."

"Did you want that? The whole college thing?"

"I never really considered it a possibility."

Because she never would have left her siblings to fend for themselves. I had to admire the family loyalty among the three of them. They'd bonded together over their shared circumstances.

Caroline stared out the passenger side window at the open water. "I don't think that route would have suited me. Not the way it will Gabi. She's brilliant."

"You're no slouch."

"No. But learning for the sake of learning's sake never appealed to me. I think I'm way too practical for that."

"The whole college thing didn't suit me either. It was why I went straight into the fire academy after high school." I glanced over at her again, gauging her mood. "Is there some other dream you've been denying yourself because of your duty to family? Something you'd really love to do?"

She stayed quiet for so long that I wondered if I'd crossed a line. "In a perfect world, I think I'd like to have a shop."

"Yeah? What kind?"

"The kind where I take the discarded things I find and turn them into something beautiful or functional."

There was probably a metaphor in there for her life, but I didn't bring it up. "Upcycling for profit. I like it. Why not do it?"

"Starting a business requires money. And I don't know if there'd be enough profit margin in something like that to justify even trying."

"It's worth doing some more research into."

"Maybe," she conceded. "Someday."

Back at the house, we made our way up the steps, noting the lack of other vehicles. "Looks like nobody's home. Do you want to come in?"

Did she honestly think I was going to say no? "Sure."

We divested ourselves of the leftovers, and I pulled her into the living room, toward the monstrosity of a sofa they'd brought home from Beachcomber Bargains. It was a hideous brown corduroy, threadbare in places, but she'd insisted she could make a slipcover that would give it new life. She just hadn't gotten around to it yet. What we *had* gotten around to was discovering that it was a damned comfy couch.

"I have a confession to make."

Her brows went up. "Oh?"

"I've been thinking very indecent thoughts about this demure little dress of yours."

I neatly tumbled us onto the sofa, so she splayed across me, her knees planting on either side of my hips. Because they were right there, I skimmed my hands up the backs of her thighs, toward her delectable ass. Caroline tipped forward, readily finding my mouth with hers, and I was lost in her, as I always was. Everything between us was heat and hands and need.

As she settled more firmly against the raging

erection in my shorts and began to rock, my blood-starved brain tried to calculate which base we were at and whether it was time to round another.

Then the overhead light switched on.

"What are you doing?"

At the sound of Rios' voice, Caroline froze. I surreptitiously removed my hands from beneath her dress.

Slowly, she sat up and glared at her brother. "We were celebrating that the Meet The Parents dinner went well."

He made a huffing noise that sounded vaguely like an enraged bull. "Celebrate somewhere private."

Then he turned and stalked off. A moment later, his bedroom door slammed.

Caroline wilted down to my chest, burying her face against my throat. "That was mortifying."

"I thought you handled it admirably. And I'm still in possession of all my limbs, so I'm calling it a win."

"Rios is protective, but not stupid. He's not going to interfere with us unless he thinks I'm not on board." She folded her arms and looked into my eyes. "He has a point, though."

"About?"

"Privacy."

"Might I point out that I live right next door?"

"And your bedroom shares a wall with my sister."

I manfully attempted to ignore how my dick jumped at the implication that we'd be doing anything in that bedroom that her sister didn't need to hear. But I didn't miss how Caroline's eyes darkened.

"You're absolutely right," I rasped, gripping her hips. "I'll see what I can do."

16

CAROLINE

"I will never not love breakfast empanadas." I bit into the tender, flaky pastry, closing my eyes as the savory, smoky flavor of chorizo and potatoes exploded on my tongue.

Across the table, Hoyt took an enormous bite of his second one and moaned appreciatively. That moan did things to me south of the border, and I restlessly crossed my legs.

"Do you know how to make them?"

"In theory, yes. But mine definitely don't beat Marisol's. She's a goddess of pastry. I'm more a buy the dough in the freezer section and assemble kind of girl."

"Valid. But maybe we could aspire to learn, because these are amazing."

I loved how he said "we" and didn't just assume that I'd figure it out because I was a woman. He was a man who liked to cook, and it had become our habit to share meals together on the days we could manage it with our schedules. Frequently, that meal was breakfast, and I adored getting to start my day with him. Even if I had been spending more and more time imagining starting that day with him in bed. His or mine. I wasn't fussy. But our schedules—and my siblings—hadn't made that possible.

Until today.

Hoyt and I had a rare full day off to spend together. As it was a weekday, Rios would be tied up with work, and Gabi was off with friends, thus leaving the house blessedly empty. Going out for a late breakfast hadn't been my plan, but when Hoyt had suggested we stop by Panadería de la Isla, I wasn't about to say no. Everything Marisol baked was amazing.

The sun was already high in the cloudless blue sky, and a lovely breeze carried the scent of the ocean past our patio table in front of the bakery. Tourists moved along the sidewalks, popping into shops or carrying coolers and umbrellas for a day at the beach. Sitting here with Hoyt, with no work on my schedule, it was almost possible to imagine what it was like to be one of them. Free to indulge in vacation pleasures. I'd never actually had a vacation. Leisure and I weren't exactly on a first-name basis. I'd always been too busy picking up the slack to take care of my family. I wondered what it would be like to have that kind of unencumbered time. Could I actually relax enough to take advantage of true time off?

"Caroline!"

I glanced up from my coffee to see Connie Galloway, the owner of Beachcomber Bargains, standing just outside the perimeter of planters that marked the edge of the patio, her goldendoodle on a leash.

"Mrs. Galloway. Hello."

"You're just the woman I was looking for."

I couldn't imagine why. "Oh?"

"I just got in a shipment of three old trunks and immediately thought of you. They'd be amazing upcycled into storage for your new place."

I blinked at the older woman, my brain already sparking with ideas. "That's great to know. I'd love to take a look at them. Thank you so much for telling me." The effort was thoughtful and unexpected. Then again, a fair chunk of all my recent paychecks and my savings had gone to her store since I'd moved out, so maybe not so un-expected.

"I'll just set them aside until you have a chance to come by. Enjoy your day with your beau." With a wink, Connie strode away, leaving me more than a little flummoxed at the easy interaction.

This wasn't the first time this had happened. Over the past few weeks, since I'd started dating Hoyt, I'd have sworn things had gotten better around town. There'd been no further action from my dad. He'd apparently decided that pretending none of us existed was preferable to acknowledging that we were adults who could make our own decisions. That was absolutely fine with us. Troy had been on his best behavior since the fire, only popping into the tavern once and leaving a massive tip. Chet and Marcus hadn't shown their faces, and no one else had said a word directly to me against me or either of my siblings. All had been quiet. Enough that my brother and the rest of his friends had somewhat backed off from the protective detail they didn't think I knew they were pulling. The only dark spots were the sporadic, small nuisance fires still popping up around the island. At this point, Chief Thompson was convinced it was troubled teens, and Hoyt hadn't wanted to talk about it when I'd asked.

Marisol came out with our check and an enormous wicker basket.

"What is all this?" I asked, eying the red-and-white checkered cloth inside.

"It's a surprise." Hoyt pulled some bills from his wallet and passed them over. "Thanks, Marisol."

"Anytime. Y'all have fun."

As she walked away, I went brows-up. "Have fun with what?"

He rose and snagged my hand, grabbing the basket with the other. "You'll see, Miss Suspicious."

Because I understood him well enough to know he wouldn't say another word until he was good and ready, I held my tongue until we arrived at the marina a few minutes later. "Why do I get the feeling you're being sneaky?"

"That is an inherent part of pulling off a surprise."

He found a parking place for the borrowed truck and slid out of the driver's seat. I waited as he circled around, because I knew he enjoyed having the chance to be a gentleman and help me down, and I'd take any excuse for him to touch me. Picnic basket in hand, Hoyt led me down a series of walkways to a slip at the far end, where a sailboat bobbed gently against its moorings. It wasn't a large vessel compared to some of the yachts that made berth here, but it certainly beat the little Sunfish I'd been on a handful of times growing up. The hull was painted a classic white, accented by the varnished woodwork on the deck. There were enough nicks and scrapes to say that this boat had seen use and was still floating, but they gave it character rather than detracting from its overall beauty.

"What are we doing here?"

"Well, we're going for a picnic sail."

I stared at him. "Is this yours?"

"Officially, no. I'm leasing it for the day, but I'd love to get one. It's a great little pocket cruiser, and this was the perfect chance to take her out for a spin to see how she handles."

Now I understood why he'd told me to wear a swimsuit this morning.

"You ever been sailing before?"

"Not on anything like this."

Hoyt stepped across from the dock, setting the basket down on the deck and offering his hand. When I hesitated, he smiled. "Don't worry. I grew up sailing. I know what I'm doing."

"I know. You were on the sailing team in high school."

His smile broadened into a grin. "You remember that?"

"I remember lots of things about you from high school. I had a terrible crush on you when I was a freshman, so I paid attention." Somehow, that was easier to admit now that we were together.

"Nice to know I wasn't the only one looking." He helped me on board and immediately stowed the basket that probably held our lunch. "Wind is good. Not too stiff, not too light. Great weather for a nice, easy sail."

And it was. With expert efficiency, he took us out of the marina, into Pamlico Sound, around the south side of the island toward the open water. I helped where I could, doing what he told me, but for the most part, I simply got to enjoy the glorious sensation of freedom that came with being out on the ocean, carried along by the breeze. It was like flying. I watched Hoyt at the helm, the wind whipping his brown hair, his teeth flashing white against a tanned face. God, he was gorgeous. And miraculously, he was mine. Maybe it was time to take that to the next level.

After an hour or so, he navigated closer to the north end of Hatterwick, on the Atlantic side. High on one of the few cliffs of the island was a big, imposing house set well away from everything and everyone else. The Sutter House, where Jace and Willa Hollingsworth's grandparents still lived. That house had stood defiant in the face of decades of Atlantic storms. What must it be like to live out here, away from everyone else on the island?

Movement on the beach caught my attention, and I gasped. "Look!"

A trio of horses plodded along the water's edge. One was clearly a baby. It dipped its nose toward the sand, then danced back as the waves lapped its hooves.

"Been a long time since I've seen any of the ponies out here," Hoyt murmured.

Like Ocracoke, Corolla, and Shackleford Banks to the north, Hatterwick had its own band of wild horses thought to be descended from wild Spanish mustangs. They mostly stuck to the hillier part of the island, which belonged predominantly to the Sutter family. I didn't know how many there were. Maybe a couple dozen? At one time, there'd been more, but their habitat had shrunk as the population of the island grew.

I leaned into the curve of Hoyt's arm. "They're so beautiful."

We watched the little trio until they disappeared over the dunes. Then Hoyt straightened and stripped off his T-shirt.

"What are you doing?"

"I thought we could go for a swim."

I glanced back at the shoreline. "Have to be extra careful here. This is where Willa Hollingsworth nearly drowned a couple of years ago."

"Oh, yeah. I guess I'd forgotten about that since I wasn't here at the time. What happened?"

I pulled off my own T-shirt, reveling in the warmth of the sun on my bare skin. "Willa's a big animal lover. She thought she saw a dog in the water and swam out to rescue it. She got caught in a riptide."

"Thought she saw?"

I shimmied out of my shorts, leaving only the swimsuit I'd put on this morning. "Well, it was night, and nobody actually saw the dog. So either it didn't make it, or she was mistaken. Either way, her parents didn't take it well. It was the same night Gwen Busby disappeared. That was what prompted them to move off island and take her with them. Anyway, Sawyer is the one who saved her. His quick thinking is the only reason she survived."

"Shit. That's gotta leave some trauma."

I thought of the watchful quiet and reserve I'd seen in Willa since she'd come to work at the tavern. She did the job, but I could tell being around all the people was hard on her. "I'm sure it does."

We drifted a little further down the coast, to the next little inlet, and Hoyt dropped anchor.

"Shall we?" He offered his hand again.

I took it, and we leapt, hitting the water at the same time. That first stunning grip of cold stole the breath from my lungs. We hadn't quite hit high summer, so the water hadn't warmed to my preferred swimming temperatures on the ocean side of the island. Kicking hard, I broke the surface and sucked in air.

"Jesus, it's freezing!"

Hoyt grinned. "Give it a minute. You'll adapt."

I narrowed my eyes at him. "A gentleman would offer to share body heat in the meantime."

"I'm nothing if not that." He reached out and snagged me, pulling me against his body.

On a sigh, I wrapped my arms and legs around him, which had the delightful side effect of settling my center against the bulge behind his board shorts. A bulge that got considerably more prominent as the motion of him treading water to keep us both afloat rubbed us together.

God, that felt good.

The low rumble in his chest told me he felt the same.

"Hoyt?"

"Yeah?" His voice was a little strained.

"Does this boat have a cabin?"

Those green eyes sparked. "It does."

"I think maybe we should go check that out instead of swimming."

"You're right. It'll definitely be... warmer below decks."

"Mmm." I gave him a quick, nipping kiss and let go, swimming back to the boat.

We clambered aboard and stumbled toward the cabin. I hadn't been inside since we boarded back at the marina, and I stopped short at the multiple little jars of flowers he'd set up in the cup holders around the space. Which meant he'd had time to plan this little outing beyond just making arrangements to rent the boat.

His hands came to my hips from behind, and he pressed a kiss to my shoulder. "Too cheesy? I wasn't counting on this, but I was hoping."

Overcome that he'd tried to add a little romance and sweetness, I turned in his arms. "It's perfect."

His lips brushed mine in a whisper of a kiss. "You're perfect."

"Mmm." Stepping away, I backed toward the double berth at the bow, reaching back to untie the straps of my bikini top. Nerves made my hands shake as the last knot pulled free, and I let the fabric fall to the floor.

Hoyt swallowed and swore reverently.

"Just so we're clear—because I know you pride yourself on being a gentleman—I want you to touch me."

"Thank God."

He closed the space between us, and then those work-roughened hands I'd dreamed about were on me, massaging my breasts, his thumbs circling my nipples until they were taut peaks. My breath hissed out.

"So damned pretty." He bent, closing his mouth around one nipple, and I wobbled as my knees went weak.

He took advantage, tipping me backward until we tumbled onto the berth, and he ranged over me, greedily suckling as he explored the rest of me with his wonderful hands. I moved restlessly beneath him as every touch and stroke lit little fires along my skin, winding me tighter and tighter. When he finally moved lower, hooking his fingers in the edges of my bikini bottoms and dragging them down, all I could think was, *Yes.*

Then he spread my thighs, settling his broad shoulders between them and dipping his head to taste my most intimate flesh.

"Oh, God!"

There was no room for anxiety, no room for self-consciousness, no room to remember that no one else had ever done this. There was only the unspeakable pleasure as he worked me with his mouth and tongue. Sensation built to an unbearable edge. My fingers clenched in his hair, and I didn't know if I was trying to pull him away or keep him close. Then he slid a finger into the center of the ache, and I detonated.

Hoyt eased me back down from the cliff. By the time the strongest of the shuddering aftershocks had passed, he'd crawled up beside me, one broad hand resting low on my belly as he stared down with a mix of wonder and satisfaction.

"I see now why we needed privacy. Need some water for your throat?"

I kind of wished for a bucket of water over my head to cool my flaming cheeks. "I... it's been a long time. And I've never done... er... that."

His eyes sparked. "Bonus for me."

Summoning muscle control from somewhere,

I rolled toward him, nipping his bottom lip. "My turn."

It took longer than I wanted to wrestle off his board shorts, mostly because my coordination was still sapped. But his amusement at that fact quickly faded when I had him in my hand. He was beautifully made, his body built for action because of his job. I stroked my thumb along the underside of his cock, enjoying how he jumped in my hand. Hoyt flailed a bit, finally coming up with a condom he'd stowed somewhere. As he rolled it on, some of my nerves came back.

I'd only done this with one other person, and not since high school. I hadn't trusted anyone enough.

At my hesitation, Hoyt lifted his gaze to me, concern all over his face. "You okay? We don't have to—"

"No. No, I'm fine. Don't stop." I wanted this. I wanted him.

He pulled me over the top of him. "You're in control."

That he'd give me this gift, understand that I'd need it, meant so much to me. I took his mouth again, sinking into the taste of sea and salt and him as our bodies heated together. Reaching between us, I notched him at my entrance and slowly sank down, using the rock of the boat to ease him deeper and deeper inside me. I was so incredibly full in the best possible way.

Hoyt's hands gripped my thighs, and the muscles of his abs shuddered. I could feel what it cost him to hold still while my body adjusted to the girth of his. Always putting me first, this man. In a life full of so many challenges, so many disadvantages, how had I gotten so lucky?

Framing his face in my hands, I couldn't quite stop the glimmer of tears. "I'm so glad it's you."

His eyes fixed on my face, and I knew the instant he registered the tears. Because I didn't want to ruin this beautiful moment, I kissed him, pouring out all the emotion brimming inside me as I began to move in a slow rise and fall, chasing our pleasure. One hand tangled in my hair, the other arm wrapping around my waist to hold me close so he could rock deeper into me with every thrust. Every nerve lit with delicious sensation. Absolutely nothing had ever felt as good as having him inside me. Each kiss grew more fevered, each touch more frantic. The wave of heat built between us until it ate through the last of our control and sent us up in flames.

Some time later, I wilted over his chest. We were both damp. From our brief swim or our own exertions, I didn't know. I just knew I didn't want to move from this spot, skin to skin and wonderfully sated. Maybe after I got my breath back in a century or so.

Hoyt stroked a hand down my spine and rasped, "Well, that seals it."

"Seals what?" I managed.

"Now I absolutely have to buy the boat."

17

HOYT

"We don't have time for this." Caroline's words were practical, but her breathy tone and the way her fingers threaded into my hair said otherwise.

I continued my slow, nibbling exploration down her throat, toward the patch of skin revealed by the V of her shirt. "I can be fast."

"Prior experience would suggest that's a lie." She hissed in a breath and tipped her head to the side as I traced my tongue along her collarbone. "Hoyt." But there was no real oomph behind what I knew she'd meant as a reprimand.

"I need you naked." I'd thought I'd spent a lot of time fantasizing about that before we'd slept together. Now that I knew what it was to be inside her, I was obsessed. Over the past week, we'd stolen what time we could, but the Universe seemed intent on interrupting us every time. We'd been playing an endless game of denied desire, and I was about at the end of my rope.

Her free hand curled around my shoulder, but she didn't push me away. "We *definitely* don't have time for that. I have work. And you have—oh God, a magic mouth."

I smiled against her skin and continued to use that mouth in an erotic assault, while I coasted my hands over her delectable ass and around to find the button of her shorts. "Let me make you feel good." Her belly tensed as my finger slipped under the edge of the waistband to graze her skin. "I know we're pressed for time, but I'm very motivated."

Her head thumped back against the cabinet, and her mug thunked onto the counter as she set it aside. "I'm not going to be able to think about anything else until you do this."

"Good." I lowered the zipper, already thinking about how wet she'd be when I slipped my fingers between her legs. My dick stirred, making it absolutely clear it was onboard with hard and fast, and let's get to it already. But before I could fulfill my promise, a knock came at the door.

I swore and dropped my brow to Caroline's. That would be my dad, who couldn't have the decency to not be early.

"I told you we didn't have time." She tipped her mouth up to mine and pushed my hands away while she zipped her fly. "You're going to finish what you started later."

I caged her against the counter. "Yeah, I am. Come to my bed tonight. Please."

Cheeks flushed, eyes huge with arousal, she murmured, "Okay."

There is a God.

Caroline glanced down at the erection tenting my jeans. "Um... how are you going to fix that before answering the door?"

My solution was to grab the tool belt I'd set on the kitchen table and strap it on like one of those sporran things Scottish dudes wore. The contents of the pouch weighed the whole thing down enough that it more or less camouflaged the situation.

Seeing the sparkle in her eyes, I fixed her with a mock glare. "Not one word."

She picked up her coffee again, her face comically blank. "I said nothing. Go answer the door before he starts to think we've been up to something."

Judging by the smirk on Dad's face, I was far too late for that. His gaze took in my no doubt messy hair and the oddly placed tool belt, and his tongue went firmly in cheek. "Mornin', son."

Hoping my expression was more sleep deprived than lust crazed, I jerked a thumb toward the kitchen. "Morning. You want coffee?"

"Sure."

Caroline had a fresh cup waiting when we got back to the kitchen. Her cheeks and lips were still flushed, but her shirt had been straightened, so she didn't look two steps away from being ravished. "Hi, Mr. McNamara. I wasn't sure how you took yours."

"Black is fine. And so is Frank."

She smiled and handed over the mug. "I'll work on it." Draining the last of her own cup, she set it in the sink. "I've gotta get to work."

I snagged her hand as she moved past me. "Where are you today?"

"I've got two rentals to clean back-to-back over on Sandpiper. Then a double at the tavern. It's going to be a long day."

I hoped she actually had the energy for my plans later. "Are you closing tonight?"

"Yeah. I won't be home until late."

"Why don't I come by right before closing? Escort you home?"

"That's really not necessary. I know you're planning a full day of reno here. Everything's been quiet, and Ed will be there."

Yeah, that quiet was part of what was bothering me. "Still. Humor me?"

"Okay." She brushed a quick kiss to my cheek. "See you tonight. Bye, Mr.—Frank."

"Bye, Caroline."

A few moments later, the front door closed behind her.

Dad smiled into his mug. "Well, that was nice and domestic."

I twitched my shoulders. "With our schedules, breakfast is usually when we manage to see each other."

"Do you have good reason to worry about her tonight? Is something going on?"

"No. Not for a while." Our nuisance arsonist had been quiet this week, leading some in the department to speculate that they'd left the island. I wasn't so sure. "I just don't like it when she closes. Last time that happened, Troy Lincoln got pushy with her. If I hadn't been there..." If I hadn't been there, stepping in and playing boyfriend, I likely wouldn't be here with her as her actual boyfriend now. But that wasn't why I intended to be there tonight. As she'd said, Ed would be there. But... "I'd just rather be safe than sorry."

"Fair enough. So, water heater replacement today?"

"Among other things. I appreciate you coming over to help. I haven't gotten as far on renovations as I'd intended."

"New relationships tend to suck up a lot of free time. But I'll warn you, your mama isn't gonna be put off too much longer. It's taken Drew and me both to keep her from just coming over here to check the place out."

"I appreciate that, too. I just wanted to get it in better shape before she saw it, so she didn't worry I took on too much."

"Oh, she'll worry about that no matter what."

"I had to shift my list around some. I originally expected to be knocking out walls first."

Dad went brows-up. "Oh?"

"I wasn't going to leave it a duplex. But then Caroline needed a place and..." I shrugged. "Here we are."

"It's a good thing you've done there, son. Above and beyond dating her. Giving all of them a place to go to get the hell out of that house and away from Hector."

"How's he been since then?" There'd been nothing from him since that one tantrum at the tavern. Rios and his friends had backed off a bit, at least from watching Caroline. The fact that she was usually with me when she wasn't at work had a lot to do with that.

"More irritable than usual. But still showing up and doing the job, so Ace has no reason to get rid of him. A good personality isn't required to be a good mechanic, and he doesn't deal directly with the public."

"I expect he's now having to do a lot for himself that Caroline and her siblings used to handle."

"Probably."

"He said anything to you about us?"

Dad shook his head. "Nah. We have a policy of just not talking unless we have to. Mostly, we don't have to. He keeps to his jobs; I keep to mine. I'm sure he has opinions, but he hasn't shared them with me."

Maybe he truly had recognized the futility of trying to control his adult children. If he wanted to be all bitter about it, that was his choice, and I couldn't give a shit. Just so long as he continued to steer clear of Caroline and her siblings. That would be one less worry.

"You ready to do this thing?"

He tipped back the last of his coffee. "Let's do it."

After verifying that Rios and Gabi were already gone for the day, I shut off the water and electricity to the house and turned on all the faucets to run out the contents of the water heater. Then I attached a hose to the base of the heater and ran it all the way out the back door. While the last of the water drained, Dad and I worked on hauling in the new one I'd picked up at the hardware store yesterday.

As we unhooked the wiring and plumbing connections, I glanced over at my dad, who'd been happily married for nearly thirty years. "Can I ask you something?"

"Sure."

"How did you know Mom was the one?"

His wrench didn't falter, though his gaze flicked up to mine. "Well, we'd been dating for maybe three months at the time. It was late spring, and I'd stopped by to pick her up for a date. I was early."

So that was clearly a lifelong habit of his.

"She wasn't quite ready yet. Said she needed to pull the laundry in before we left. I followed her outside. The sun was shining down through the trees, and it hit her hair just so while I watched her gather all these sheets that were billowing in the breeze, putting them into a basket. That moment just struck me right in the chest, and all I could think was, 'Yeah, I want this for the rest of my life.'"

He finished loosening the connector. "Maybe that's stupidly sexist because it was a woman folding laundry. But it wasn't about the laundry. It was this incredible, domestic sort of vision that made me think of home and comfort, and I knew she was going to be at the center of it. And she always has been."

Folding his arms across the top of the water heater, he fixed me with a look. "You having one of those moments?"

I thought of how Caroline had looked the day we'd gone sailing. Not straddling me in the cabin —though that would always rate among my top favorite memories ever—but before, when we'd been cutting through the water. She'd tipped her face up to the sky, eyes closed as the wind whipped her hair and she'd looked so... free of all the burdens of her everyday life. It had struck me right down to the marrow that I'd done that for her. That I wanted to keep doing that for her for always.

"Yeah."

Dad nodded. "Thought you might. You've got the look."

"The look?"

"Like you've been whacked over the head with the love stick."

I snorted. "The love stick?"

"Stupid term for a serious condition. You in love with Caroline?"

I didn't have to think about it.

"I am. I know it's fast, but that's where my head is. I'm good at looking into the future. That's why I bought this house. I can see what it will be when I'm done. Now, when I look out into that future—five years, ten years, twenty—I see her. Is that crazy?"

Dad smiled. "No. I'd say that's just love. You told her yet?"

"No. I don't want to freak her out. Our whole relationship has been, in some ways, faster than I think she's entirely comfortable with, so I'm gonna sit back and let things take their course. Wait until I don't think the idea of it will scare her to death."

"Sensible. For what it's worth, your mom thinks Caroline looks like she's been hit by the love stick, too. And she's usually a pretty good judge of these things."

That gave me a jolt. "What does she think about it?"

"That you'll give her beautiful grandbabies if she keeps her nose out and doesn't say things like how you'll give her beautiful grandbabies."

I laughed outright. "Okay, yeah. Good call on her part. That would *definitely* send Caroline running. She's spent her whole life taking care of her siblings. I don't know how she feels about the idea of a family of her own someday. I don't even know how she feels about the idea of marriage. For her, I think that's all way on out there in a hazy future. And that's okay. We've got plenty of time."

"But you're gonna fix up this house with that in mind?" Dad prompted.

"Damned straight."

"Solid plan. Let's swap out these water heaters."

18

CAROLINE

"I swear, we're trapped in some kind of time warp." Willa laid her head on the bar top I'd just wiped clean.

I glanced at the clock. "Only another forty-five minutes 'til closing."

"Can't come soon enough."

Gently, I tipped her chin up so I could look at her face. Her skin was pale beneath the tan she'd acquired since coming back to Hatterwick, and her eyes were hugely dilated. "Girl, you look awful. What's going on?"

"Been fighting a migraine for the last hour or so."

"Shit, Willa. Why didn't you say something? You should've gone home."

"I didn't want to leave you handling everything by yourself, since Ed didn't make it back from the mainland."

Our boss had gone over for his second doctor's appointment in as many months to get the results of some kind of tests. I didn't know for what, but given he'd been over there hours longer than expected and had missed the last ferry back, I was starting to worry it was something serious.

"You're a sweetie. Thank you."

"Bartenderrrrr."

I turned toward the slurred voice at the end of the bar to find its owner pointing to his empty glass, asking for another refill. The guy had been parked on that stool for the past two hours, with one brief break to go out and take a smoke on the patio. Not a local, which I would've known even if he hadn't shared his girlfriend woes with me in great detail over the course of way too many drinks. They'd had a fight, and she'd stormed off, taking the car. He'd wandered in to soothe his bruised ego. I'd been keeping an eye on him, and it was clear he'd had enough. I knew what he was going to ask, and I knew how he was going to react when I said no.

Bracing myself for confrontation, I filled a

glass with water and moved on down the bar to set it in front of him.

The guy stared at the water with bleary, unfocused eyes before lifting his gaze to mine. "That'sssss not what I ordered."

"Nope, but you've had enough for tonight."

"What? No, I'm good. Just one more."

"We're just one more'd out. I can't serve you any more alcohol, for your safety and everybody else's." I nudged the water closer to his hand. "Time to sober up a bit so you can get safely back to your rental."

His face reddened, and he banged his fist on the bar hard enough that the utensils on an uncleared plate further down the bar rattled. "This is bullshit! I know when I've had enough. Give me another bourbon!"

The remaining handful of patrons went so silent, I could hear my own quickened breathing.

Threat.

I felt the scream of it in my head as adrenaline dumped into my system, but I knew I had to stay calm. Dealing with intoxicated customers was always a dicey proposition, and I really freaking wished Ed were here or that Jasper weighed more than a buck fifty.

"I'm sorry, sir. I really can't. It's our policy. Why

don't you work on that water while I cash out your tab?"

His anger simmered just below the surface, his glare fixed on me. I kept my gaze on his, aware of every minute movement in my peripheral vision. This kind of situation could turn in an instant, and the last thing I wanted was trouble, especially as I was the thing keeping everyone in the bar safe right now.

"I. Said. Another. Bourbon," he repeated, his voice rising with every syllable.

This was not going to go well.

Shifting to the balls of my feet in case I had to move fast, I kept my own voice steady. "I'm really sorry, but I can't do that. And if you don't calm down, I'll have no choice but to call the police."

He stood up so fast, his stool clattered to the floor. "You can't tell me what to do!"

In an ideal world, Hoyt would've chosen this moment to come through the door. But I wasn't expecting him for another half hour or more. I was in this on my own. My hand inched down the bar toward the phone.

"You need to leave. Now." Despite how shaky I felt, my tone was firm.

His hands balled into fists, and he took a step

closer. "You're just a little girl playing bartender. What are you gonna do about it, huh?"

I didn't have a choice. This was likely to get ugly. Grabbing the phone, I held it up so he could see. "You have a choice. You can take yourself out of here on your own, under your own steam. Or you can continue to act like a jackass until the police arrive and they escort you off the property. You don't have to go back to your rental, but you can't stay here."

The air crackled with tension. I had no idea what he would do, and my finger hovered over the keypad, ready to dial 911, even as my muscles tensed, ready to move if he lunged at me.

At last, he spat out a curse and staggered toward the exit, pushing open the door so hard it slammed against the outer wall. I flinched at the crash.

Silence reigned for a few more moments, but the asshole didn't come barreling back in. I exhaled a slow sigh of relief, setting down the phone with shaking hands. I glanced at the last table of customers, offering a weak smile to reassure them and myself that all was well. But my heart still thundered in my chest.

Look at that. A shit situation and you handled it. You didn't need Hoyt.

But damn, I'd wanted him. It had been nice having a big, strong man step in a few times, so I didn't have to.

"That could have gone very badly," Willa murmured.

"Yep."

"What about his tab?"

"I've got his credit card. No doubt, he'll realize that tomorrow and come back to get it, but for now, we're going to close it out and call it done." Taking another calming breath, I turned to the girl. "You go on back to your place. Take some headache meds. Curl up in the dark."

"I don't want to leave you here by yourself."

"I'm not going to be by myself. Jasper is here, and Hoyt is coming by any minute now to escort me home. It'll be fine. In fact, as soon as this table is ready, I'll close them out, too, and lock the doors. Ed will understand if we close a little early tonight."

Willa bit her lip. "Are you sure?"

"Absolutely." I gave her a gentle squeeze. "Go rest and feel better."

As she disappeared through the back to clock out, I picked up the pitcher of tea and went out to the last table of patrons, a group of four forty-something women who were on their annual girl's trip. The redhead, who seemed to be their appointed leader, just lifted her hand in a staying gesture. "No, we're good. I think you have the right idea closing early. You handled yourself really well there."

I offered a tired smile. "Unfortunately, it comes with the territory. Let me get y'all your checks."

Willa was gone by the time I'd closed out their table and escorted them all to the door.

"Y'all have a good rest of your vacation!" As soon as they were out, I turned the lock and felt about a hundred times better. Raising my voice so Jasper could hear, I announced, "We're closing early!"

The cook stuck his head in the window between the bar and the kitchen. "Thank God. I have a date tonight."

That reminded me of the plans I had with Hoyt later. God, I hoped I actually had the energy. At this rate, I wasn't sure I'd be able to stay awake, no matter how magic his mouth was.

Heading to my locker, I pulled out my cell and sent him a quick text.

> Me: Closing early. Come around back when you get here.

I didn't get an immediate reply. Maybe he was tied up with something. I knew he and his dad had been hard at work tackling a lot of projects around the house. By this point, he might've been in the shower cleaning up from his long day. He'd be here by the time I was through.

Smiling to myself, I slid the phone back into my purse and went to start the closing routine. Before anything else, I closed out Mr. Belligerent's tab. David Foley was probably going to have a minor fit at how big a tab he'd run up. But that was what happened when you numbed your issues with top shelf alcohol. I ran the credit card he'd left, then placed the card itself in the cash drawer, locking it safely away until he returned for it.

After dealing with Mr. Belligerent, the quiet stillness of the bar was welcome. Wiping away the remnants of spilled drinks and scattered bits of food was almost meditative. As I worked, the sharp scent of cleaner gradually cut through the lingering odors of alcohol and grease that permeated the air. From the kitchen, I could hear Jasper shutting down the grill and oven, the clanging of pots and pans providing a staccato rhythm for my own work. Gathering up the final empties, I loaded glasses into the dishwasher and started the cycle. I'd still need to restock the beer fridges and wipe down the bottles lining the shelves, but that could wait a bit. I wanted to finish with the dining room first.

Moving methodically around the space, I turned chairs up and onto the tops of tables, clearing the floor for a sweep and mop. We'd been busy tonight, and there'd been spills. Best not to leave that for Bree tomorrow when she opened.

Jasper was hauling the garbage out when I walked into the back hall and opened the closet to retrieve the mop and broom. Whoever had last used the rolling mop bucket had just shoved it in here. Multiple brooms and other detritus had fallen over. I took half a step inside to begin untangling the mess when something hit me hard between the shoulder blades.

I cried out, crashing into the mess of handles. Pain lanced through me as I hit the floor at an awkward angle and something else banged into my head. The door swung shut behind me, leaving me in sudden darkness.

"What the actual hell, Jasper?"

I upended the mop bucket as I scrambled to my feet, shins throbbing where I'd landed. If this was his idea of a practical joke, I had a foot that was just ready to shove up his ass. I reached for the handle to open the door, but it didn't turn. "What the fuck? This is not funny! What the hell are you thinking?" I jiggled it harder, throwing my shoulder against the door to pop the lock. It wasn't a fancy one. It should've given way. But even when I hurled my full weight against it, the door stayed shut tight. Something was wedged against it on the other side.

The first true hint of worry began to leech through the anger. "Jasper?"

There was no answer.

I might not have been Jasper's favorite person, but he wouldn't have done this. Which meant... what? Had someone attacked him when he went outside with the garbage? Were we being robbed? Had David Foley come back?

Shouting Jasper's name, I began to kick at the door, trying to open it. But I got no further than I had with my shoulder. This looked so much easier in the movies.

Okay, calm down and listen. The police will want to know what I observed.

I went still and strained to hear anything going on outside the closet. But there was nothing. No sound of voices or footsteps. No sound of anything.

Please let Jasper be okay.

Maybe I could see something through the

crack under the door. Shoving cleaning supplies aside, I got down on hands and knees and attempted to peer out into the hall. I didn't see anything.

But I smelled the acrid tang of smoke.

19

HOYT

I thrust my hands beneath the running water and scrubbed them with mechanic's soap for the third time. "How is it there's not yet a better way to get caulk off of hands?"

"It's one of life's greatest mysteries," Dad agreed. "Sometimes you just have to let it wear off."

Given my plans for the night involved running these hands all over Caroline, I was highly motivated to get the rest of the crud off. Maybe scrubbing was the wrong tactic. Perhaps something oily would help?

"I'll figure it out. You head on home. I'm sure Mom is waiting to interrogate you about the house. I gotta clean up and get on into town to meet Caroline."

"Will do."

"I appreciate all your help today, Dad. Truly." It hadn't been a visibly productive day, but we'd gotten tons done. After changing out the water heater, we'd gone through the house and caulked every damned thing that could conceivably need caulking. Trim. Doors. Windows. All necessary before doing the more fun stuff like painting. I was glad I had one more day off before being back on shift. My hands were already cramping like a son of a bitch. They'd need a chance to rest.

He clapped a hand on my shoulder. "Anytime. You bring your girl back around the house. Your mom and I like her."

"I'll do that."

After another two rounds of scrubbing, I'd gotten the worst of the caulk off. I could still feel the pull of it on my skin, but at least my hands were clean enough I could actually check whatever text had come in earlier.

Pulling the phone from my pocket, I found a message from Caroline.

"Closing early," I muttered. Shit, this message was from twenty minutes ago.

I elected to forego the shower and headed

straight into town. Maybe I could talk her into a joint one when we got back home. There were a few fantasies that had been keeping me up nights that I'd love to enact.

As she'd instructed, I circled around back and parked. Her car and one other were still in the lot. Good. Then I hadn't missed her. Shutting off the engine, I slipped out of the truck. The moment I did, I smelled the smoke.

"Caroline!" I bolted for the building, one hand already reaching for my phone to dial the fire-house, when I spotted the feet sticking out beside the dumpster.

Heart in my throat, I poured on more speed, skidding to a stop and falling to my knees. Not Caroline. Jasper. He lay facedown on the pave-ment, blood matting the hair on the back of his head. I called it in, even as I checked for a pulse. The thrum beneath my fingers reassured me he was just unconscious. I didn't even register who answered the phone before I was barking into it. "This is Lieutenant McNamara. There's a fire at the tavern. At least one victim of blunt force trauma out back."

I heard the wail of the alarm bell, both over the phone and in the distance. They were only a couple of blocks away. They'd be coming fast. Thank God.

I was dimly aware of the man on the other end of the phone warning me to stay put as I hung up. I knew protocol. Knew the dangers. And I didn't give a damn because Caroline could be in there. As I circled the building, trying to assess the state of the blaze, I cursed the arsonist who'd taken out my truck. All my personal protective equipment had burned up with it. I had only myself.

"Caroline!"

There was no answer.

The awning windows hadn't yet been shut for the night. Smoke was already beginning to billow out the side. I boosted myself through one of them, dropping instantly to the floor. The fire hadn't yet reached the dining room, but the smoke was getting thicker. Yanking the bandana I'd been using as a sweat rag all day from my pocket, I tied it over my face and began moving toward the kitchen. I could see flames creeping up the walls through the pass-through. Once they got to this side and reached the alcohol, everything was gonna go up like tinder. Why the hell hadn't the fire suppression system kicked on? The building was equipped with sprinklers.

I kept shouting for Caroline, scanning the floors, terrified of what I might find.

The swinging door leading into the kitchen was hot to the touch. If I opened it, I'd be giving the fire more oxygen. The smart move was to wait for backup and get the hell out of here.

Then I heard the faint sound of pounding over the roar of the flames. That wasn't outside.

"Caroline!"

Was that shouting? It had to be. The thumping got louder.

In the back of my brain, I knew the engine should be here by now. They'd be unfurling hoses, getting lines going. So I took the risk and kicked open the door.

Flames reached for me with greedy fingers as I hurled myself through the opening. The smoke was thicker here. My skin prickled from the heat as every drop of moisture evaporated. Coughs racked my body as I struggled to figure out where the noise was coming from. The office? The cooler? Why couldn't I hear the pounding anymore?

That was when I spotted a metal chair wedged beneath the knob of another door. No way was that an accident. The hallway beyond it was fully engulfed, a gaping maw leading straight to hell.

But I didn't hesitate. I leapt toward the sink and the bar towel draped over it. Damp, thank God. Then I went straight for the belly of the beast. Kicking the chair away, I reached for the knob with the towel. Even through the extra fabric, I could feel the sear of heat, but I managed to get it open.

Caroline was crumpled to the floor amid a mess of cleaning supplies. She'd wedged a wet mop beneath the edge of the door to block the smoke. Smart girl. But she wasn't moving. Terrified, I scooped her up just as something exploded.

Shit!

The fire had reached the bar area and all that alcohol. Turning quickly, I realized the way I'd come in was blocked. Both our escape routes were covered up with flames.

Suddenly, the back door splintered open, and familiar helmeted shapes were coming through the door. The one in the lead waved for me to come on, even as water was being directed against the flames. Eyes stinging, chest burning, I hurtled out of the building and away from danger.

Someone tried to take Caroline from me, but I clutched her close. At least, until another coughing fit took me down to my knees. Somebody put an oxygen mask over my face. I started to shove it away, to push it toward Caroline, but I realized they'd done the same for her. And her eyes... those beautiful, bloodshot eyes were open. Thank God.

I reached out a hand and snagged hers, relieved to feel her squeeze my fingers.

Looking back at the building, I saw multiple lines being run. They'd be prioritizing keeping the fire from spreading to buildings beyond. I didn't know if any of this one would be salvageable by the end. But Caroline was okay. That was the only thing that mattered right at this moment.

Abruptly, she sat up, tugging off the mask. "Jasper! Where's Jasper?"

"He's out." I spotted him being treated a couple dozen feet away. "I found him knocked out by the dumpster, but he's alive."

Caroline scooted closer and slumped into me. "Thank God. You came."

"Of course I did. I always will." I wrapped an arm around her. "What happened?"

She started to speak and fell into another round of coughing, then had to wait for a little more oxygen. "We closed early. It was just Jasper and me left. He'd gone to take out the trash, and I was about to go mop the dining room. Somebody shoved me into the closet and blocked the door somehow."

"They'd wedged a chair under the handle." And now that I was out of the danger zone, the full implication of that began to sink in.

This fire hadn't only been arson, it had been attempted murder. And Caroline had been the target.

20

CAROLINE

The sun was cresting the horizon by the time we made it home from the island clinic, where Hoyt and I were both treated for smoke inhalation. There'd been a raging debate about whether we ought to be transported to the hospital at Nag's Head, more for Hoyt than for me, as his injuries were worse than mine. Ultimately, he'd insisted he was fine, and he knew how to treat the second-degree burns he'd sustained. Because he'd *rushed into a burning building with no gear to save me*.

I was still processing that and pretty sure I'd fall apart about it later when the numbness of exhaustion had worn off. Judging by the crowd of vehicles at the house, that wouldn't be anytime soon. I didn't recognize all of them, though I knew at least a couple belonged to Sawyer and Ford, who'd come over to stay with Gabi while Rios was with me at the clinic. But the fire chief's truck and the police cruiser were obvious enough.

I'd known I'd be questioned about last night. But I'd passed on as much information as I could to the firefighters on the scene before we'd been taken to the clinic, so I'd hoped there'd be a chance to rest before going through everything again. No such luck.

Hoyt and I were both moving slowly as we slid out of his father's SUV. He'd been the one to stay with us all night. Rios had already parked his car on the shoulder of the drive and raced around to meet me. I waved off his effort to help me up the stairs. Everything hurt, but I was getting inside under my own power. Hoyt needed to see that I was okay so that he'd sit his ass down and rest himself.

Gabi flew out of our apartment. "Caroline!" She raced over to me, skidding to a stop inches from touching me.

I worked up a tired smile. "I won't break, *hermanita*." When I opened my arms, she came into them, squeezing me tight. It hurt, but I just held on because she needed the reassurance.

Her eyes were welling with tears when she pulled back. "You smell like smoke."

"Yeah. Haven't gotten the chance for a shower yet." Though the nurse at the clinic had managed to dig up some scrubs for me to change into. That had helped a little, but the scent still clung to my hair and seemed to emanate from my pores. I wasn't sure a single shower could wash it away.

"Chief Carson and Chief Thompson are here."

"Of course they are," Rios muttered.

"It's procedure," Hoyt said. "Let's get this over with."

We all trooped inside to find not only Ford and Sawyer but also Drew, standing like a sentinel. Ibbie hovered, a dishtowel in her hands as she frowned at the two unwelcome guests. The moment her eyes lit on Hoyt, she dropped the towel and rushed to him, stopping at the last second, as Gabi had.

"I'm all right, Mom. Promise."

Her lip trembled as she spotted the bandages covering his burns. "But your hands."

"Nothing that won't heal." He pulled her in for a hug. "Thanks for holding down the fort."

"Of course."

He'd called his family to be with Gabi, too?

Circling the wagons to protect us. My throat went tight that his family was willing to do that for us.

"We're sorry to invade like this. We know you've had a long night," Chief Thompson began.

Bill Carson made a rude noise and folded his arms. He looked older than his forty-something years, with hair that was more iron gray than brown and a lined face that had been prematurely aged by years of wind and sun. That face was full of derision as he looked around the home we'd made, watching my brother prowl the room like a caged animal.

How much of that tension was because of the police chief's presence and how much because of what had happened to me?

Thompson shot an impatient look toward his police counterpart. "I know you made a statement at the scene, but I'd like to go through things again, in case you remember anything more."

"Of course," I rasped.

"We're going to sit." Hoyt herded me over to the sofa, where we both lowered down. Why did I feel like I was eighty years old?

"Do you want some tea?" Ibbie asked.

"Just water. Thanks." My throat was raw from the smoke, and would be for a while.

As she disappeared, Rios looked to Ford and Sawyer. "Any word from Jace?"

"He's at Willa's. She's good."

My head jerked up. "Is there any reason to think she shouldn't be?"

"Just precaution," Ford reassured me.

The Wayward Sons doing what they could to protect their own.

Ibbie came back with glasses for both Hoyt and me. I clutched mine in my hand, sipping gingerly.

"Take us through it at your own pace. What happened last night?" Chief Thompson prompted.

"It was a reasonably slow night. I was on my own with Jasper Bolton, our cook, and Willa Hollingsworth, one of our servers. Ed was on the mainland for an appointment and missed the last ferry back." I told them about my altercation with David Foley and how I'd decided we would close early after that.

"Did he threaten you?"

"He was aggressive, clearly wanting to beat on someone, but he didn't actually touch me. There were no explicit threats where he announced he'd do something to me if I didn't do what he wanted, but he was very agitated."

Thompson made notes on the little notepad he

carried. "Did you see any sign of Foley after he left the bar?"

"No. But I wasn't looking outside. After the last customers left, I locked the main door and started to clean up." Step-by-step, I went over everything I'd done, all the way through getting shoved into the supply closet.

"Did you hear anything after that?"

"No. I was shouting for Jasper. For a minute, I thought he'd pushed me in as some kind of stupid prank. But then I couldn't get out, and I smelled the smoke."

I closed my eyes as remembered terror washed through me. Trapped, with flames creeping up the walls mere feet away on the other side of that door, with no way to know if anyone would make it in time.

A warm hand closed around mine, grounding me. Hoyt. Always Hoyt. Mindful of his injuries, I didn't let myself squeeze back, but I laced my fingers with his.

"I don't know what happened outside that closet until Hoyt found me."

"Convenient," Carson drawled.

I stiffened. "Excuse me?"

"It's the second fire you're connected to that you mysteriously don't know anything about.

Somebody might think you've got it in for your employers."

Hoyt nearly exploded off the sofa. "She didn't lock herself in the goddamned closet and levitate a chair underneath the door handle to lock herself in. Someone tried to kill her. Get your head out of your ass and work this case properly instead of letting your personal prejudice get in the fucking way."

Carson scowled. "Watch yourself, boy."

This time, Hoyt did stand. Drew and Thompson were both there to block him from access to the chief of police.

Thompson maintained his reasonable tone. "Sit back down, Hoyt."

Hoyt's shoulders were heaving as he glared daggers toward Carson, but at length, he sat.

"Clearly, she didn't set the fire herself. That's objectively impossible. We're looking for someone else. But it's possible there could be a connection to you. That it might be a hate crime directed toward you and your family. Both the beach house fire and this one strike at your means of income. It's possible that someone is trying to drive you off island. Can you think of anyone who'd want to do that?"

Over the past two years, we'd faced so much

hatred and prejudice. But had anyone seemed so determined that they'd go to this much trouble to get rid of us?

"Not that I can think of. A lot of people have made snide remarks or been outright ugly to all of us. But no one seemed angry enough to do something like this."

"What about Chet Banks? You had some kind of run-in with him and Marcus Hoffman."

I glanced at Hoyt. "It wasn't exactly me who had the run-in. I make it a policy not to react, but Hoyt defended me to them and got into a verbal altercation." That felt like a lifetime ago.

"And Troy Lincoln?"

"We've had him under surveillance since the vehicle fire," Carson interrupted. "He wasn't anywhere near this."

"Are you sure?" Thompson prompted. "Have you spoken to the officer assigned to watch him? Or have you slacked off since everything's been quiet until now?"

"Don't tell me how to do my job, Thompson."

"I'm just pursuing all avenues. Lincoln wanted Caroline and was pissed she chose Hoyt. Could be he wanted some kind of payback."

Wasn't that a cheery thought?

"That doesn't fit with the beach house fire," Carson insisted.

"No. It's likely we're dealing with more than one perpetrator. Right now, we're trying to get at the details that will help us evaluate which fires were likely set by the same one." Thompson turned back to us. "Is there anyone else?"

I thought of the horrible scene from the day my father had confronted me at work. "Our father." I outlined what had happened that day, again citing Hoyt's defense. "But he's steered clear since his blow up. I guess he's disowned us."

"Fine with me," Rios muttered.

"Well, you're just making enemies left and right," Carson sneered. "Guess it runs in the family."

Hoyt shot up again, vibrating with rage. "Get the fuck out."

Carson didn't even flinch. "I've got everything I need, anyway. I'll be in touch." The chief of police turned in the doorway. "And don't leave town, Miss Carrera. You're a person of interest in this case."

"You son of a bitch—"

This time, Rios and Drew caught Hoyt before he could fly at Carson.

The older man looked at Frank. "I'd think

you'd be worried about the company he's keeping. Sure seems to be having a bad influence on him."

Thompson sighed. "Carson, get out of here and stop antagonizing my witnesses."

"Just remember which of us is in control of this investigation."

Everyone in the room held their collective breath as he strode out of the house and thumped down the steps.

Hoyt rounded on my brother. "Were you not going to say a word to defend her?"

Before I could open my mouth to say how out of line that was, my brother responded with admirable calm. "That man wants to put me away for a murder I didn't commit. I can't afford to antagonize him."

Hoyt's nostrils flared. "You're right. I'm sorry."

"Doesn't mean I wouldn't like to plow my fist into his face."

"I'll hold him down," Hoyt snarled.

"Maybe don't be plotting an assault on an officer. You're no good to me in jail," Thompson said mildly.

Hoyt spun toward him. "Tell me you didn't hear everything he just said. He's not going to take this investigation seriously. He's going to blow this off and point it toward something else, just because he doesn't like Caroline's family for God knows what reason. We can't let that happen."

"We won't. We'll continue to run our own investigation, separate from the police department. We're going to find out who did this."

I appreciated his intent, but I was losing faith.

Because it seemed like maybe the questions were over for now, I finally asked the one that had been circling around my brain since we'd left the scene. "How bad is the tavern?"

At the fire chief's hesitation, my heart sank. "We won't know for sure until we get a structural engineer in to confirm it's safe to do further investigation, but we know the control valve for the sprinkler system was damaged. That's why they didn't turn on. There's no question this was arson. We'll be checking out David Foley to find out where he went when he left the bar last night. We'll also be speaking with Ed Cartwright to see if he's had any problems with anyone who might target the tavern. It could be a coincidence that you happened to be there. We've had multiple fires on-island this summer, and not all of them had anything to do with you directly or indirectly. So we're going to keep looking. In the meantime, Hoyt, you are officially off duty until further notice. Rest. Heal. Take care of each other. We'll keep in touch."

Frank shook the fire chief's hand. "Thanks for looking out for my boy. For both of them."

Then he was gone.

"Well, that was some shit."

I had to admire Drew's tendency to cut through the niceties to get to the heart of the matter.

Hoyt sighed and sank back to the couch beside me. "It's been a long damned night. Thank y'all for coming out for us."

"Always, brother."

Rios finally stopped pacing, moving over to settle into one of the folding camp chairs that were the only other seating we had. There were still things to discuss. Long-term ramifications of last night's events, and it was obvious he knew it.

Ibbie fidgeted in the living room doorway. "Do you want something to eat?"

Hoyt's stomach let out a growl in answer to that. "I could eat."

I wasn't sure if I could, but if she was kind enough to put food in front of me, I'd sure as hell try. "Some breakfast would be great. Thank you."

Hoyt's mom wrapped an arm around Gabi's

shoulders. "Come on, honey. Let's put together some food for everybody."

As soon as they were out of earshot, I dropped my voice to a near whisper. "I have no idea how we're going to keep afloat after this."

Rios reached out to squeeze my shoulder. "I've got some put by. And you'll find another job."

I hadn't even begun to process the reality of that. Because regardless of the degree of damage to the tavern, chances were it would be closed the rest of the season. And that was if Ed decided to rebuild. Maybe he'd decide it was too much. Maybe with whatever he had going on with his health, he'd elect to retire. Either way, that didn't solve the immediate problem.

"Who's going to want to hire me? I'm lucky that Mr. Foster didn't fire me from my cleaning job."

"You had nothing to do with that," Sawyer defended.

I lifted my gaze to his, then to Ford's, and back to my brother. "But think about it. Carson's not actually wrong about this. One of the properties I clean caught on fire and is still being repaired. Now the tavern? Regardless of whether this is bad luck or if it's directed at me or our family, seriously, who is going to want to hire me after this? Who would want to risk it?" As the fresh fear began to take hold, my throat tightened. "I don't know how we're going to afford rent, groceries, anything."

Hoyt wrapped an arm around me. "We'll make it work. I don't need the rent. Put what you've got toward essentials right now. It'll be fine."

How the hell was it going to be fine? It wasn't reasonable for him to have to pay for his association with me. That was what all this felt like. No amount of arguing could convince me that the burning of his truck wasn't somehow connected to me. What was going to be next? I closed my eyes as every single doubt and worry I'd had about getting involved with Hoyt ignited again.

His lips brushed my temple. "Don't you dare. This is not your fault."

Of course, he knew where my head was going.

I blinked back tears. I'd managed to hold them in all these hours, but now, my head ached and my throat was raw from smoke inhalation and too much talking. "I'm so tired," I rasped.

"Go to bed, sis. Get some rest. We'll talk about everything when you wake up later."

I didn't know that things would look any better on the other side of sleep, but the idea of a few hours of attempted oblivion sounded like heaven. But first, a shower.

When I shoved up from the couch, Hoyt rose with me.

"No. I want a shower and a few hours alone."

I registered the flash of hurt in his eyes and turned away before I caved. The seams of my control were fraying, and I didn't want him there when they ripped. That wasn't an intimacy I wanted to share with anyone. Not even him.

I made it up the stairs on my own. But as I turned on the water and stripped down, I couldn't stop myself from considering the realities of what came next. We were free of our father. Maybe it was finally time for all of us to cut our losses and consider leaving the island.

No matter who we'd be leaving behind.

21

HOYT

I stared after Caroline, feeling like I'd just been kicked in the gut. Somehow that hurt worse than the burns, worse than my raw throat and gritty eyes. It didn't take a genius to see she was pulling away. That she'd taken everything Carson had said to heart and was blaming herself for all of this. And I didn't know how to make it better for her. I didn't know how to stop her from blowing us up in some deluded attempt to protect me.

Fucking Carson.

I'd never had reason to like the man, but I'd never truly despised him before. I did now. If he cost me Caroline...

"Lock it down," Rios murmured.

I glanced up at the younger man, seeing the same rage simmering in his eyes. Something passed between us. An understanding we hadn't had before. Sucking in a breath, I nodded.

Somehow I made it through shoveling in the breakfast Mom and Gabi made us, though I didn't taste a thing. I let Mom fuss long enough to reassure herself I was really okay, then I claimed exhaustion—not a lie—and sent my family home to get their own rest.

The moment they were out of the house, Gabi seemed to deflate. "I'm going up for a nap, too." She crossed over to me and slid in for a careful side hug. "Thank you for saving my sister."

I'd never had a sister, but I found hugging her back wasn't awkward. "Anytime."

Her smile was a little wobbly around the edges. "You're one of the good ones, Hoyt."

"Thanks?" What else could I say to that?

She moved around the room, hugging Ford and Sawyer, in turn, before moving to her brother. Rios gave her a tight squeeze and sent her off with a murmur of something in Spanish that I didn't understand, but held clear affection. None of us spoke as she trudged slowly upstairs. I considered making my own exit, but I understood Rios had things to say to me. Maybe I did to him, too. And I knew his friends were here to discuss next steps.

"You really care about her." Rios's soft voice wasn't full of surprise or question. He said it as a calm statement of fact.

No pulling punches or pussy footing around it, then. That was fine. I didn't have the energy for anything but straight shooting.

I turned to face him. "I'm in love with her." No sense in hiding it. My actions last night had spelled it out clearly enough.

His steady gaze showed no surprise. "Have you told her?"

A million times in my head. "No. I'm not sure that would help the situation right now. She thinks she's bad for me, all because of that fucking son of a bitch, Carson."

The smile Rios flashed was bitter. "He's certainly not winning any popularity contests with me."

Too tired to keep standing, I dropped into one of the camp chairs. "Why does he hate your family so much?"

Ford leaned against the wall. "That's the million dollar question."

"One I don't have the answer to," Rios continued. "I don't know if my dad did something to him or if he's just a racist son of a bitch who sees a brown man as a convenient scapegoat."

"Fucker. Nobody with that kind of prejudice should be in any kind of position of power."

"You're not wrong. We're not going to fix a broken system. But I do have some insight into my sister."

"Lay it on me. I'll take whatever advice I can get."

He leaned forward, bracing his forearms on his knees. "She's somebody who takes everything on herself, and she's gonna be taking this pretty hard. This was all shit she was worried about before she got involved with you, so it's just pressing on existing fears. If she tries to push you away, don't let her. Stand your ground. She's stubborn. All of us are. If you really want to be with her long-term, then you've got to be patient enough to weather that."

Waiting? Hell, it felt like I'd been waiting for Caroline Carrera my whole life. What was a while longer? Especially now, when I knew what it was to be with her. "I can do that. I can give her the time she needs and just be here on the other side when she's ready."

"Good. Now go to bed yourself. You look like you're about to drop."

He wasn't wrong. I'd already been dragging from the adrenaline crash after the fire. Having a second round from my confrontation with the chief of police hadn't helped.

"What about keeping tabs on the girls? I know we slacked off on that, but now..."

"We'll take care of it," Sawyer said.

And I had a moment to realize that Rios and his friends were a true unit. They operated together the same way I did with my fire crews. As a team. Or in their case, a family. They'd take care of their own.

Reassured by that, I hauled myself around to my side of the house and made my way upstairs. Though every step felt like moving through quicksand, I took the time to shower, washing away the remnants of smoke that still clung to my hair and skin. All my burns woke up and screamed at the lukewarm water. Gritting my teeth, I got through it, refreshing the burn cream and bandages before preparing to fall into bed.

But I couldn't make myself do it. Not just yet. Stepping out on the balcony, I strode around to Caroline's door. If she'd been just a tenant, this would cross a line. Probably. But she wasn't just a tenant, and I couldn't rest until I saw she was okay. Peering through the gap between the sheers she'd hung over the French door, I saw her curled up on the air mattress, her damp hair curling across the pillow. Her chest rose and fell in a slow, easy rhythm. Sleeping.

Reassured, I trudged back inside and collapsed onto my bed. Sleep took me under fast.

Gasping for breath, I stumbled through the thick, choking smoke, the searing heat of the flames wrapping me in a hellish embrace. "Caroline!"

The fire roared like a living beast, hungry and merciless. I stumbled on, the fear of not finding her a knife in my gut.

The dining room was fully involved, flames dancing with a terrifying frenzy up the walls, across the ceiling. Each step was a battle against the heat that threatened to consume me. My skin felt like it was melting, the bandana over my face useless against the smoke that clogged my lungs.

I pushed through to the kitchen, the door hot to the touch. The flames reached for me with greedy fingers, a wall of fire blocking my path. The heat was unbearable, a physical force that pushed me back.

The sound of Caroline's voice was faint, a ghostly whisper over the crackling fire.

"Caroline, where are you?" I choked out.

Smoke blurred my vision, and my eyes streamed. I couldn't see her. Couldn't figure out where the screams were coming from. Everywhere I turned was more flame, and I realized that the fire had closed in, cutting off any exit.

I hadn't found her, and now we were both going to die.

"Caroline!"

"Hoyt, wake up. I'm okay. I'm safe. Wake up."

I rocketed out of sleep, already reaching toward Caroline's voice. And there she was, kneeling beside me, one hand on my shoulder. My arms closed around her. Real. Alive.

"You're okay. You're okay." I gasped it over and over, my voice ragged.

She wrapped around me. "You got me out. I'm fine." The rasp of her abused throat was music. "You were having a nightmare."

That pulled me the rest of the way out of the dream. Judging by the angle of the sun, it was much later in the day. Was it the same day? Or had I managed to sleep into tomorrow? Had she? We'd gone to bed separately. She'd shut me out.

Remembering that, I loosened my hold. "What are you doing here?"

"I woke up a bit ago. I was out on the balcony,

and I heard you. You'd left your door unlocked, so I thought I ought to wake you up."

"Thank you." Remembering that she'd said she wanted to be alone, I reluctantly let her go. "I promised I'd give you space."

She pulled back far enough to look at me. "Do you want space?"

"Hell no. I want you right here." Where I could feel her, safe and whole.

"Okay, then." She gently pushed me back into the pillows and stretched out beside me, snuggling close.

The knots in my chest loosened. I wasn't sure if this meant she was done taking her distance, or if she was staying for my sake until I settled. Grateful for her presence either way, I brushed a kiss to her temple. "Were you able to sleep?"

"Some. You're not the only one who's having nightmares. I expect that'll last for a while."

"Probably. But we're gonna be okay. We're going to get to the bottom of all this." I tightened my hold on her. "None of this was your fault."

Her sigh tickled the side of my throat. "It feels like my fault."

"The only person at fault for any of these fires is whoever struck the match. You're not responsible for any of their behavior or motivations. That's akin to victim blaming."

"Fair point." She lapsed into a weighty silence, and I wondered if I needed to press any harder.

When she spoke again, her voice was barely above a whisper. "I was all set to leave the island."

Every muscle in my body tensed. "What?"

"That's what I was lying in bed thinking about. How if I left, maybe all of this would stop, and innocent people would stop getting hurt."

It took me a few moments to recognize that the frantic gallop of my heart was panic. "You don't know that."

"No, I don't. And it occurred to me that if that happened, if it were true, that I'd be giving whoever this is exactly what they want. I'm not in the habit of giving in to bullies. But that wasn't what changed my mind."

She'd changed her mind. Did that mean she was staying? "What did?"

She propped herself up so she could look down into my face. Her fingers stroked feather soft along my cheek, the pads of her fingers catching against my stubble. "I'm selfish."

"You're one of the least selfish people I've ever met."

Caroline huffed a humorless laugh and shook her head. "It turns out I can't walk away from you."

For a few moments, all I could feel was the tangle of relief and nerves and hope in my gut. "Why?"

Those big dark eyes stayed steady on mine. "Because I'm in love with you."

I didn't move, lest I find out I was dreaming again.

Her smile was rueful. "I think I was always a little bit in love with you. Or at least the idea of you." That pointer finger traced my jaw. "The reality is so much more than I imagined. So much more than I ever thought that I could have. And I don't want to give that up. If that makes me selfish, so be it."

Her mouth came to mine, soft, soothing, and I threaded my fingers into her hair, hanging on. "If you'd left, I would've followed."

She pulled back again, far enough to look down at me. "Why?"

"The same reason I violated every bit of my training and ran into a burning building with no gear to save you. Because I love you."

I watched the wonder break in her face like the dawn, and I wanted to see that look every day for the rest of my life.

"Hoyt." Her eyes were wet with unshed tears, but this time I knew they were happy ones. She deserved so many good things in her life, and I wanted to be the one to give them to her.

I drew her down again, taking her mouth in a long, drugging kiss that inevitably sparked into more. Her hands skimmed down my bare chest and lower, hesitating at the waistband of my sweatpants.

"Don't stop."

"You're hurt."

"Nowhere it matters."

That was all the invitation she needed. She bent, trailing kisses down my torso as she scooted lower and lower, dragging off my sweatpants. It was a novel thing, having her strip me first, torturing me with her mouth and hands until I was one step above feral.

Surging up, I rolled, pinning her beneath me. "Need you." I needed to feel her around me. Needed to remind us both that we'd survived.

She wrestled out of her cami top and the little shorts she'd slept in until she was bare to my hungry gaze and ravenous mouth. Then it was my turn to drive her up, up, up, until she was chanting my name, begging for more.

We had just enough mutual sanity left to remember the condom. She ripped the packet open, rolled it on. Then I plunged into her, burying myself inside that sweet, hot body over and over, drinking in every gasp, every moan, and demanding more, until we both flashed over the edge together.

22

CAROLINE

Two days after the fire, I stood with Hoyt on the sidewalk in front of the tavern and stared. From the front, you almost couldn't tell anything had happened, other than the lingering scent of smoke in the air and the caution tape that had been strung up to keep the curious away. Not that it stopped the Lookie Loos from hanging out at the perimeter. Plenty of them had stopped to gawk. More than one looked our way as we ducked beneath the tape and made our way around to the back.

The full reality of the devastation hit me like a physical blow as I took in what remained. The kitchen, once full of life and warmth, was now a gutted shell. Charred remains of what had once been counters and appliances were scattered amidst the debris. The stink of burnt wood and melted plastic hung heavy in the air, a stark reminder of exactly what Hoyt had risked his life to pull me out of.

My heart sank as I stepped closer. The wall that had separated the kitchen from the bar and dining area was almost entirely gone, reduced to a few crumbling pieces of plaster and exposed beams. I could see straight through to where the bar once stood, now just a blackened, unrecognizable mess. The dining room, though not as badly damaged as the kitchen, bore the scars of the fire, too. Soot and ash covered everything, and the tables and chairs were upended, some reduced to charred fragments. The back side of the building housing the supply closet where I'd been trapped was straight up gone.

There was absolutely no question in my mind that if he hadn't come after me, I would've died in there. The memory of the dark and the smoke and the heat made me shudder.

Hoyt wrapped an arm around me. "Okay?"

"Yeah."

There was more activity back here. I spotted Ed, his face gray beneath his beard, his eyes devastated. This was his life's work, reduced to ashes.

How could I face him after this? And yet, I owed him that respect.

Bracing myself, I closed the distance. "Ed?"

Those lines of strain on his face eased a little when he spotted me. "Caroline."

I swallowed against the knot in my throat. "I'm sorry." The words slipped out, hardly louder than a whisper. My voice was still a rasp from smoke inhalation, but this struggle was more from grief and shame.

"Oh, honey, no. This isn't your fault. I'm just so glad you're all right." He pulled me in for one of his gruff bear hugs, and I leaned into it, feeling unworthy of this good man's absolution.

When he released me, I fought back emotion. "I don't know what your plans are, but I'm there to help in whatever way I can."

"I appreciate that, darlin'. We haven't been cleared to start cleaning up the damage yet. Hoping to get in soon, though. That fella over there is an arson investigator." He jerked his head toward where a man I didn't recognize was poking through the rubble while Chief Thompson waited nearby.

"How did we land an arson investigator this fast? I thought they had to come from off-island." I was sure Hoyt had mentioned that after the beach house fire.

Hoyt stepped up. "We've had so many fires this summer, we finally got moved up on the list. He'll probably be checking out the beach rental, too."

Across the parking lot, I spotted Bree and Ford. Tears tracked down her cheeks, and as I watched, Ford took her into his arms. She burrowed into him, burying her face against his broad shoulder. He pressed a kiss to the top of her head, holding on as she cried.

It was a Thing that Bree was letting herself lean on him. She liked to pretend she didn't need anyone—a sentiment I more than understood. I hoped that at least one good thing could come from this nightmare. Maybe Ford would realize he felt more for her than mere friendship.

Beside me, Hoyt hadn't stopped scanning the crowd, his body tense.

"What's wrong?"

"Just watching everybody, noting their reactions."

"Why?"

"Frequently arsonists will come back to see the results of their actions."

Well, that was a chilling thought. The idea that the person who'd tried to kill me could be nearby, watching us all. I looked over the gathered crowd myself. Chet Banks was at the edge of the perimeter, staring at the damage. His eyes fell to me, and his expression shifted to an angry glare, as if I'd been the one to set the fire. Or maybe like he was sorry I'd made it out?

I stepped closer to Hoyt. Troy Lincoln was there, too. I knew he worked nearby. It was why he'd frequented the tavern so often. His office was only a couple of streets over. I couldn't read his face, and I wondered what he was thinking.

There were tourists there, too. I saw a couple of teenaged boys I recognized as summer people. They'd become regulars around town over the past couple of months. Seemed like I remembered something about how their parents were professors or something and had booked one of the rentals for the entire summer. A frenetic energy fairly crackled around them as they stared at the damage. Did that mean something? Or was it just that this was the most exciting thing to happen on this usually quiet island since their arrival?

"He found something," Hoyt murmured.

I turned in time to see the arson investigator rise from where he'd crouched in the wreckage, putting something into a container.

"Whatcha got?" Chief Thompson asked.

The investigator stepped free of the debris and walked over. "Maybe the thing the perp used to start the fire. This look familiar to any of you?"

He held out the heavy-duty plastic evidence bag. Inside was a silver square, warped from the heat. I realized after a moment it was a lighter. There were marks on the surface.

Hoyt spotted those, too. "Can I see that, sir?"

The investigator handed him the bag. We both peered closer, trying to make sense of the lines. They'd blurred some, but they were still mostly legible. It was a set of engraved initials.

DF.

My heart kicked up in realization. "David Foley. The drunk guy who got aggressive with me the night of the fire. The one I kicked out. He'd been smoking earlier. I didn't see his lighter specifically, but what are the chances that another lighter with his initials would be here in the rubble?"

Jaw set, Thompson pulled out his cell. "We'll have him brought in. We definitely have some questions."

23

HOYT

I stared at David Foley through the one-way mirror, taking in the khaki shorts, pink polo shirt, and well-worn Sperrys. His blond hair was tousled in a way that looked too deliberate. This guy belonged on a country club golf course somewhere or schmoozing over corporate lunches. Entitlement practically oozed out of every pore. I had a hard time imagining him getting his hands dirty. But looks could be deceiving.

Had this pretentious fucker been the one to circle back the other night to lock Caroline in that closet because she'd dared to tell him no? Had he attacked Jasper, then used that lighter to start the fire and just left her to die?

Chief Thompson closed a hand over my shoulder. "Keep it together, son. By rights, you shouldn't be here after that blow up with Carson yesterday."

That was true enough. I was surprised the chief had agreed to bring me when I'd asked to tag along for the interrogation. Caroline had stuck around with Ed and Bree to help coordinate clean up, as the arson investigator had said they could get back in that afternoon. I knew Ford would keep an eye on her, and it seemed like we might have our perp right here.

The door to the interrogation room opened, and Chief Carson strode inside. He dragged out the only other chair in the room across from Foley at the rickety table and sat.

"Appreciate you coming in, Mr. Foley."

"Am I being charged with something?"

Oh, hell. Was he about to lawyer up and stonewall us?

"No. We're just asking some questions, trying to get a better picture of what happened the night of the fire at the OBX Brewhouse. You were one of the last folks to leave, so we wanted to find out if you remembered anything."

Foley's shoulders relaxed a fraction. "I don't remember much. I'd been drinking pretty heavily that night before I left to walk back to my rental."

Carson nodded. "Why were you drinking that night?"

"I'd had a fight with my girlfriend. But we've sorted everything out now. It's fine."

The police chief made a show of checking the notes he'd brought with him. "Says here there were a few people there who reported you got a little aggressive before you left the bar. That you didn't appreciate being cut off."

Given how little Carson thought of Caroline, I was actually surprised he'd even asked.

Foley ducked his head, a bit of color rising in his cheeks. "Yeah. I was probably a dick. I think I scared the girl on duty." That head snapped back up. "But I didn't do anything."

"Sure, sure." Another consultation of the list. "You ever been to Hatterwick before?"

Blond brows drew together. "Yeah. Why?"

"When was that?"

"Earlier this summer. Back in early June. I was here with some friends for a bachelor weekend."

Carson was nodding. "You remember where you stayed?"

"In a rental over on Sandpiper something or other."

I tensed, waiting to see where this line of questioning would go. I remembered Jim Foster reporting that the beach house had been left a total disaster. Was that a result of a bachelor party gone a little too wild?

"Whose name was the rental under?" Carson asked.

"Lucas Platt."

"Shit," I muttered. "This was one of the last people inside that house before it burned." Maybe Carson wasn't quite so shitty at his job as I'd believed.

In the interrogation room, I could see Foley starting to tense up again. "What are you getting at, Chief?"

"Well, it happens that the last time you were here, there was a fire in that rental. Same day y'all left." Carson opened a folder he'd brought in and pulled out photos from the scene of the beach house fire.

Foley blinked. "We had nothing to do with that. We were gone."

"Right, right. I'm just wondering if you remember seeing anything that morning. After all, y'all were there. Not a lot of other folks in the area."

The other man threw up his hands. "No. Why would I? It was weeks ago."

"The thing is, David, you were here on-island

right around the time this beach house burned. And now you're back on-island at the same time the Brewhouse burned."

An angry flush worked its way up Foley's neck and into his face. "I didn't *do* anything. I'm sure lots of people were on-island at the same time as both those things."

"True enough." Carson placed the evidence bag with the lighter on the table. "Do you recognize this?"

Surprise flickered over the other man's face. "That's my lighter. I lost it when I was here earlier in the summer. Where did you find it?"

"Lost it, huh? Didn't report it."

Foley looked at Carson like he was an idiot. "It's a lighter. Why would I report it? It's not like you would have done anything. I assumed I left it behind. Clearly, someone found it."

"Mmmhmm. Well, the problem here, David, is that multiple witnesses state you got pretty aggressive with a bartender on duty last night when she refused you service. And it doesn't look good for you that somebody locked her in a supply closet after closing and used this very lighter to set the place on fire. That just seems like one too many coincidences to me."

The guy was starting to sweat. "I want my lawyer."

"I think that's a pretty good idea. Because here's what it looks like to me: You were here earlier this summer, maybe realized you forgot your pretty lighter. All engraved with your initials and shit. Seems like it was a nice one. Maybe a gift from your girl? Something that means something to you. Anyway, you realized you left it and came back to the house to retrieve it."

Foley fisted both hands on the tabletop. "I don't know anything about any fires. I didn't go back to the house. Hell, if you want to talk to somebody who's into that shit, look for the kids who were there that week."

"What kids would those be?"

"There were some boys in the rental next door. High school age, I think. I saw them screwing around with some fireworks, setting a trash can on fire. Maybe they found my lighter. I don't fucking know, but I didn't do this."

Carson closed his folder and rose. "We'll do that. In the meantime, why don't you get in touch with your lawyer?"

When he walked out, I looked at Thompson. "Do we have rental records for the rest of the area around the house?"

"One of the officers put them together."

"You think those teenagers are still here?"

"I don't know, but we damned sure need to find out. If what he says is true and they're still here, they might be responsible for a bunch of these nuisance fires this summer."

"Maybe. But there's a big damned difference between the small shit like trash cans and mailboxes, and knowingly burning down an occupied structure. Hell, even if the teens were here and were responsible for some of the chaos, I don't see them escalating like that. And actually, I'm not sure I can see Foley doing it, either."

Michael studied me. "You trying to talk us out of suspecting this guy?"

"No. Just thinking." I tried to imagine where his head might have been. "He was drunk. Angry at women in general. Got cut off by Caroline and kicked out of the bar. That would've stuck in his craw, been embarrassing. He'd have gotten more angry, might've wanted some payback. But I can't quite make that fit. I could see him setting fire to the building after everybody was gone. But there were still cars in the lot. It was obvious people were still there. No matter how drunk and pissed this guy was, I can't see him attacking Jasper and deliberately locking Caroline in that closet. He doesn't have any priors. Someone capable of that kind of violence wouldn't fly under the radar so easily." And he didn't have the dead eyes I would expect in someone capable of murder.

Michael folded his arms. "Foley could've snapped."

"Maybe." I certainly wasn't an expert in psychopaths. "Or it could be that he's telling the truth. That he lost the lighter when he was here earlier in the summer. The perp could have found it and has been using it. He might've left it behind at the tavern fire either by accident or in a deliberate effort to frame Foley."

The pieces just weren't quite coming together.

"We've thought all summer we were dealing with more than one perp," Michael pointed out. "Whether Foley's guilty of this fire or not, it's possible he's giving us some answers to some of them. Let's see if they're still on-island and go from there."

I followed him out of the observation room and into what counted as the bullpen of our tiny island police department.

As soon as Carson laid eyes on me, he glared. "What the hell is he doing here?"

My boss didn't even blink. "Just observing.

What's the word on those teens? Is it possible they're still here?"

Officer Chris Shelton looked up from a pile of paperwork. "According to rental records, there's a family who leased one of the houses for the entire summer. Both parents are professors, and they've got two boys. The house they rented is two doors down from the one that burned."

Carson was already moving toward the door. "Then let's find the little bastards and bring them in for a chat."

24

CAROLINE

I eyed the stairs up to the house, gauging whether I'd be able to make it up them. Everything hurt, all the way down to my hair. My body letting me know in no uncertain terms that I'd overdone it this afternoon. But the tavern had been cleared for cleanup, and I'd leapt to help Ed and Bree start the process. We'd still been picking through the rubble, searching for anything salvageable, when the huge construction dumpster had been delivered. Along with it came more helping hands. Neighbors. Friends. Other island business owners. Hatterwick was coming together to help one of its own.

Ed had taken this blessing in stride, maintaining his stoic demeanor. But when the remains of Marv, his taxidermied marlin, had been discovered, he finally broke down. That damned fish had been his pride and joy. Seeing him standing amid the charred remains of his business, tears streaming down his weathered cheeks, my heart broke right along with his.

But we were going to build it back, and it was going to be better than ever. It had to be. Any other outcome meant that the bad guy won, even if he went to jail.

I had to think that was what would happen to David Foley. The police had hauled him in for questioning, and Hoyt had gone with Chief Thompson to observe. I hadn't heard a word from him since, which said to me that Foley was still in custody and the questioning was ongoing. Tying up loose ends, I supposed. But his lighter had been found on the scene. Surely that meant he was responsible.

"Need a hand?"

I continued to eye the stairs, even as I waved Rios off. He'd picked me up from the tavern and brought me home when he'd gotten off work. "I'll make it. No reason for you to get filthy, too."

I was covered in soot and grime. The clothes I'd been wearing were probably ruined. But it had been worth it to take positive steps toward

cleaning up, even though the actual rebuilding
would be a long time out. I was desperate for a
shower and food and about a gallon of water.

It was the lure of the latter that finally got me
up the steps and into our apartment. Rios poured
me a tall glass, so I didn't actually touch anything.
He even dragged out one of the wooden crates we
were using for stools at the kitchen table.

Grateful, I sank down, feeling every ache of my
muscles. "Thanks."

He handed me a couple of painkillers. "Here.
This will help."

Dutifully, I tossed them back and guzzled
down the water.

He refilled my glass, then took a seat beside me
at the table. "Do you think it's finally over?"

"God, I hope so. Hoyt's still at the police station, so far as I know." I could only imagine what
had been happening with the investigation for the
past few hours. No doubt the cops would have
searched Foley's rental looking for additional evidence. I knew from Rios's experience that the police could hold Foley for quite a while without
actual charges. But there'd been no direct evidence tying my brother to Gwen's disappearance.
That lighter might as well have been a smoking
gun.

But I didn't bring any of that up. I didn't want to risk making Rios relive any of the shit he'd dealt with when he'd been taken in for questioning. "What will you do if it is over?" It was something that had been circling around in my brain since Hoyt had asked me what dream I'd been putting off.

"What do you mean?"

"Gabi will leave for college in a few weeks. We're out of Dad's house. You're not bound here anymore. You don't have to stay for me. You've got the chance to go somewhere else. Do something else. Start over."

Rios hesitated, not quite meeting my eyes. "I was considering going into the military. Actually, we all are."

I blinked in surprise. "Really?"

"Yeah. Sawyer has nothing left here now that his dad's gone. Jace doesn't want to follow the path laid out for him by his parents. Ford... Well, he's looking for a different direction. And you're right. I want a chance to start over." He brought his gaze to mine. "I feel more okay about the idea of taking that chance now that you have Hoyt." His lips curved a little. "I like him for you."

I smiled back. "I like him for me, too."

Knowing what a big deal this was for him to

even consider, I laid a hand on his arm. "I am fully in support of you getting to have your own life. If this is your path, you should take it."

His shoulders jerked in a shrug. "Well, we'll see. There's still time."

His phone vibrated with a text. He glanced at the screen. "Gabi's done with work. Apparently, Lisa got a flat and can't bring her home. They need a rescue. Do you want to come with?"

"I really, *really* want to shower. And you don't want to put this back in your truck." I waved a hand to encompass my general filth.

"I don't like leaving you here by yourself."

"The most likely suspect is already in custody. I'll lock up. It'll be fine. You won't be gone that long. And when you two get back, we can spring for pizza for dinner." It was a rare treat, but I thought we'd all earned it.

"That is definitely a plan." He rose. "Lock up behind me."

I followed him to the door and did exactly that. Once he heard the lock snap into place, he saluted and trotted back around to the front of the house. As his truck pulled out of the drive, I grabbed a trash bag and made my way upstairs and into the bathroom. In truth, I was relieved to have a little time completely alone. There'd been someone around all the time for most of the summer. A safety precaution organized by my brother and Hoyt, I knew. A sensible one, at that. But the quiet, empty house was rather lovely.

Stripping off my grimy clothes, I put them straight into the trash bag. I would attempt to wash them, but I didn't have a lot of hope. Maybe Hoyt would have some laundry secrets to getting soot out of fabric. The shower was hot, and as I didn't have to worry about conserving water for anyone else just now, I lingered, scrubbing all the black from my skin and out of my hair. When I was through and the last of the gross circled down the drain, I decided to really indulge and run a bath. I'd have a bit of a soak. That would surely help my sore muscles. Plus, it would be easier to shave. My mood had picked up considerably, and I wanted to celebrate the probable end to all the insanity when Hoyt finally came home. So I'd take the time to scrub and buff and moisturize, doing everything possible to make myself utterly touchable. He'd enjoy exploring every inch with his hands, and I'd enjoy the consequences of that. Win-win for us both.

I was just finishing up with my legs when my phone vibrated with a text. I checked the screen.

Rios: This is gonna take a bit
longer than planned. You may
not want to wait dinner.

That was fine. I was still enjoying my alone time.

Feeling a little playful, I took a careful shot of my bare feet propped up on the edge of the tub and texted it to Hoyt.

Even as the message sent, I heard a noise from downstairs. Obviously, Rios wasn't home with Gabi yet. The only other person who had a key was Hoyt himself. Grinning to myself, I tapped out another text.

I can hear you downstairs. Rios
is out helping Gabi and a friend
with a flat. Why don't you come
up and join me?

Then I tossed the phone aside. I wished I'd thought to start some music, maybe pull out some candles. Or maybe not. I wasn't sure I'd be okay with open flames any time soon. But we didn't need all the trappings to enjoy each other.

On a sigh, I settled back into the water, relaxing against the back of the tub.

Footsteps sounded on the stairs. Slow, a little heavy. Sounded like he was tired. It had been a long day for him, too. Maybe I'd talk him into stripping down and letting me pamper him for a change.

The door swung open slowly.

"I've been waiting for you."

When Hoyt didn't immediately respond, I cracked open my eyes and glanced toward the door. In the shadows, I could only see the hulk of broad shoulders, but something about his posture seemed... off somehow.

Concern cut through the playful as I sat up. "Baby, what's wrong?"

The figure just outside the doorway stepped into the room.

Not Hoyt. Not safety. It wasn't over yet, and I was utterly screwed.

The man in the doorway smiled because he knew it, too.

I screamed, though there was no one else around to hear.

25

HOYT

The interrogation room was getting crowded. Carson had brought in Damon and Eric Bradford, along with their parents, Doug and Nicole. Someone had dragged in a couple more chairs, but there still wasn't enough seating for everybody, especially not once both Carson and Chief Thompson stepped inside.

Yet again, I was being allowed to watch from the observation room, provided I didn't interfere. I wanted this whole thing done by the book so that if these little shits were guilty, they wouldn't weasel out of the consequences. And judging by the evidence collected in the initial search of the property by Sutter's Ferry PD, they were guilty of something.

"Our boys didn't do anything," Doug Bradford insisted.

"They're good kids. Honor roll students," Nicole added.

"As we said back at the house, if they're innocent, then there's nothing to worry about in a search. Y'all were incredibly cooperative. We really appreciate that." Carson sounded almost amiable. "You've been on-island all summer, so you know we've had some trouble, and we're eager to get to the bottom of it."

Doug Bradford was the picture of agreeableness as he nodded, his salt-and-pepper hair hardly moving a millimeter. "Understandable. Which is exactly why we let you search the house."

I didn't miss how Damon, the elder of the two boys, jolted at that announcement. Eric's face paled.

Yeah, you had something to hide that Mommy and Daddy didn't know about.

"We found some interesting stuff." Carson put three evidence bags on the table. He tapped each one in turn. "Firecrackers. Lighters. Lighter fluid."

"That doesn't mean anything," Doug insisted. "I smoke, so the lighter and lighter fluid are mine. And we bought firecrackers for the Fourth of July."

Carson nodded. "Sure. That makes sense. One

of my officers also found this in the outside garbage can." He added a large plastic bag to the table. Inside was some kind of fabric. An item of clothing? I couldn't tell from where I watched. "Seems like those are scorch marks on this hoodie."

Damon lifted his head in defiance. "I caught it on the top element of the oven when I was pulling some tater tots out the other night. Since there was a hole in it, I didn't see the point in keeping it."

But Eric's shoulders were creeping up around his ears.

Nicole's expression was turning mutinous. A similar shade to her eldest son. "I don't like any of what you're implying, Chief Carson."

Carson smiled, but there was no hiding the edge to it. "I don't like the mess somebody's been making of my island." He set one last evidence bag on the table. Inside was a cell phone. "This is one of those new-fangled models with the facial recognition. I'm a fan of having a fingerprint or proper password myself, but it's handy in cases like this." He pulled it out of the bag and tapped the screen on, then held the phone up first to Damon's face, then to Eric's. The screen unlocked. With a few more swipes of his fingers, he opened some app on the phone and set the device down on the table.

I didn't have a good view from here, but I could see shades of red and orange on the screen. Flames?

Carson swiped the screen, moving from image to image. "If your boys are such law-abiding little angels, how is it they've got pictures of what appears to be every fire set on this island since the start of the summer?"

Eric's face had turned a little gray.

Damon stared at him. "You dumb fuck. You took pictures?"

"Damon! Language!"

Doug clearly wasn't registering the implications of what was happening.

But his wife was staring at her youngest. "Eric, explain yourself."

The boy's shoulders were rounded, and his voice was so soft, I almost couldn't hear it. "It was Damon's idea."

Yeah, throw your brother under the bus.

Everyone turned to stare at Damon. I could see him considering the wisdom of doubling down, but ultimately, he threw up his hands. "Yeah, okay, fine. We set a few trash cans on fire. Some mailboxes. It was no big deal. Just little stuff."

The elder Bradfords erupted.

"Why would you do such a thing?"

"How could you?"

"Don't say another word. We're getting you an attorney." This last came from Daddy.

Eric seemed to shrink further in his chair. Nicole's face was ashen as she studied her oldest son. "What were you thinking?"

Damon's shoulders jerked in a belligerent shrug. "It was just something to do. We've been so damned bored here. There's absolutely nothing to do on this backwater island."

Chief Thompson had been standing quietly in the corner, observing the proceedings, but at this, he stepped forward. His jaw was granite. "Do you have any idea how many resources you wasted this summer? How many lives you risked by tying up the fire department with these nuisance fires? We're the first line medical response on this island."

Tears were tracking down the younger boy's face now. Damon seemed to be dialed to a hundred percent defiant.

Their parents appeared to have the good grace to be horrified.

"How could you do this?" Doug demanded. "You're supposed to be a better influence on your brother."

"I shouldn't have to be my brother's keeper. Why did you have to bring us to this place? Taking us away from our friends and everything there is to do?"

For all his bluster about a lawyer, Doug Bradford seemed to finally register that they were fucked. "We're happy to pay for damages. Both of them will be grounded until the end of time, and certainly they'll do community service to help make up for everything."

Carson was back to looking conciliatory. "I appreciate that, Dr. Bradford. I do. But it's not that simple. There are the criminal charges for the house they nearly burned down, and the truck they torched. Not to mention the destruction of the OBX Brewhouse a couple days ago."

At this declaration, both kids went sheet white.

"We didn't have anything to do with any of that," Damon insisted. "We were at the house with our parents the night the tavern burned."

"Can anybody other than your parents verify that fact?" Carson asked.

"Actually, yes. We had company over for dinner that night," Nicole said. "We were all playing games until right before they left around ten."

"We'll need their names and contact information to verify. But that doesn't clear you of the rental fire at the beginning of the summer or the vehicle fire a few weeks ago."

"We didn't burn either of those." Damon's expression turned speculative. "But we know who did. That was what gave us the idea in the first place."

"If you know anything about either of those fires, you'd best speak up right the hell now, son," Carson warned.

"I want immunity."

"This isn't the movies, kid. You're not getting jack shit when you've already confessed. Now, unless you want to go down for these other two fires, I'd start talking."

Apparently realizing his little gamble wasn't going to get him anywhere, Damon lost some of the bravado. "Our rental is a couple of doors down from the one that burned. We saw a guy sneaking out of the house after the guys who'd been there that weekend had already left. I noticed because he looked older than the dudes who'd been staying there, and I thought it was a little weird. Then we saw the smoke."

"Why didn't you call 911?" Nicole's voice had gone strident.

Another shoulder jerk. "We wanted to see what would happen. Nobody was there. The hotties cleaning the place had left."

Caroline and Gabi. I wanted to plant my fist in the little shit's face.

"Can you describe the guy you saw?" Carson asked.

"Big guy. Broad shoulders. Dark hair."

Which could describe about fifty percent of the men on the island at any given time.

"Anything else?" Thompson prompted. "Anything about what he was wearing?"

"We didn't get a good look."

"He was scruffy," Eric added. "Like he hadn't shaved in a few days."

"What about how he was acting? Where he went after he left the house?" Carson prodded.

"Not after, but before. He came from the house across the street," Eric said.

"From inside that house?" Thompson asked.

"No. Like he'd been hanging around outside somewhere. But out of sight. I think he was waiting for those cleaning ladies to finish and leave."

The perp had been watching Caroline and Gabi. I curled my hands into fists, wishing these kids could give something actually useful.

Carson leaned forward, bracing his hands on the table. "This is really important, kids. Have you seen this guy at any other point this summer?"

Eric nodded. "On the street behind the fire station. It was the day that truck got set on fire. We were wandering around town and saw him slipping out from between some buildings."

"And how did you know it was the same guy? Maybe it was just somebody who happened to be cutting through the alley."

"Because we could smell the gas on him. It's not a smell you forget."

Again, not evidence it was the same person, though it did link whoever they saw the second time to my truck.

"Did you get a better look this time?" Carson asked.

Damon squinted, thinking. "He was wearing a baseball cap and sunglasses. Older guy. Maybe a little older than Mom and Dad. Kind of weathered around the face, like he spends a lot of time outside. He walked right by us. We pretended not to see because we recognized he was bad news."

My brain spun. If these kids were responsible for all the smaller fires this summer, and this second perpetrator had torched the beach house and my truck, what were the chances he'd been the one behind the tavern fire, too? I considered what little they'd said about him. Dark hair. Scruffy or bearded. That narrowed it down. Troy, Marcus, and David Foley all had lighter hair and were generally clean shaven. Of the two remaining, only one actually looked older. Except, he'd had an alibi for when my truck had been torched, so the cops had stopped looking at him.

Had a coworker lied for him? Or had they simply assumed he was where he was supposed to be, when he was supposed to be there?

Either way, Caroline needed to know that the threat definitely wasn't over.

I yanked out my phone, intent on calling to warn her, and spotted her text.

> Caroline: I can hear you downstairs. Rios is out helping Gabi and a friend with a flat. Why don't you come up and join me?

The message came with a shot of her feet, clearly in the bathtub.

Fear grabbed me by the throat as I hit her contact and listened to the phone ring and ring before

it finally went to voicemail. I bolted out of the observation room so fast that the door banged
against the wall.

Someone was in the fucking house with her,
and she thought it was me.

26

CAROLINE

Terror chilled my skin despite the steaming bathwater. I was achingly aware of my vulnerability, naked, with no weapon and my only route of escape blocked by a man who'd made my life a misery.

I hadn't been truly alone with him for years. Rios had seen to that.

Once, I'd put all my energy into being what he wanted. Tiptoeing around his temper, never doing anything that could set him off, because I was the one who looked most like our mother, and he hated her for leaving him. He'd used his fists on me to remind me of it often enough until Rios had gotten big enough to fight back.

I'd thought I was free. That I'd finally broken loose of his hold. But as my father watched me with glittering, hate-filled eyes, I understood that I'd only delayed the inevitable. That he was determined not to let me go. In the back of my brain, I'd known it had been too quiet. I'd known he'd accepted the situation without nearly enough fight. But I'd let myself fall into the fantasy that I could actually have this new life I was building with Hoyt. I'd deluded myself into believing he wasn't a threat.

Now, I was going to pay for that foolishness.

But I'd be damned if I'd let him see my fear. "Get the fuck out of my house."

Hector shook his head. "It's not your house. You're spreading your legs for that McNamara boy rather than taking the home I gave you. A whore, just like your mother."

I hadn't thought I could feel more naked than I already was, but at his words, I curled in on myself. Not out of shame for giving myself to Hoyt, but because everything about this was inappropriate. Hector had never sexually assaulted me, never shown any signs of crossing that line, but he was *looking* at me in a way that made my skin crawl.

Desperate to cover myself, I surged up and

grabbed the robe I'd left on a chair, dragging it on. It was the only thing within reach. Why the hell had I tossed my phone away? I could see it on the rag rug in front of the sink, where it had landed. If I could manage to get to it, somehow dial 911...

Hector didn't move, only shook his head. "I knew you were planning to leave. Ungrateful bitch. After everything I've done for you. A daughter should honor her father."

At the outrageous declaration, I almost laughed. But I didn't dare antagonize him further by pointing out all the ways in which he'd failed as a father.

"But no. You forced me to sneak around rather than obeying as you should. I tried to block you, but nothing worked. Foster didn't can you for the fire. And that bastard McNamara apparently didn't clue in that you were more trouble than you were worth. Guess you're just that good a lay. I gave you one last chance, and you ignored it. So I'm done with you and your lack of respect. Your lack of gratitude."

All the spit in my mouth dried up as he dragged his gaze over me. The wet robe was no real barrier to the perusal, but I clutched the lapels tight together over my breasts. This man had committed arson in the name of trying to get me back under his thumb. He'd tried to take out my means of income and the emotional support system I'd found in Hoyt.

Had he somehow been behind the tavern fire, too?

"What do you want?" I hated that my voice trembled, hated that he noticed.

"I want you to pay for leaving me, just like your mother did."

The words struck me almost as hard as a physical blow. "What are you talking about?"

Mom had left him. Left all of us. She'd been so afraid of him, she hadn't risked taking us with her when she ran. And she'd never looked back. Never even tried to contact us again.

His lips curved in a cruel, satisfied smile. "You didn't think I actually let her make it off the island, did you?"

I was shaking now with more than fear, as all his terrible implications sank in. "What did you do?"

"I gave her a choice. She chose wrong, so she learned what you're going to—No woman leaves me."

"You killed Mom," I whispered in horror. That

was what he was saying. He'd murdered her rather than allow her to live a life without him.

Hector inclined his head. "It was pitifully easy. She was weak. And she thought she'd be able to sneak all of you away without my knowing?"

The emotional hits just kept on coming. Mom had intended to take us with her?

"I couldn't allow her to do that. You're my children. My family."

In another man, the words might have felt good. To be claimed. Wanted. But this wasn't that. This was some twisted form of possession. Not love.

"Where... where is she?"

He jerked a shoulder. "At the bottom of the Atlantic. Or maybe in the belly of a shark. It was kind of a letdown, really."

A letdown. As if murdering his wife, the mother of his children, and disposing of her body in the ocean was akin to throwing back a fish that wasn't up to standards.

His eyes hardened. "I had more interesting things planned for you, but you got lucky. Your little hero showed up and went running in after you. But he won't be saving you this time. He and the police are all chasing their tails, thinking it was that rich white guy. I knew that lighter was going to come in handy."

My father was behind the tavern fire. He was the one who'd shoved me into that closet and barred the way out. He'd already actively tried to kill me once, and now he was here, determined to finish the job. No way would he be running his mouth this freely if he intended for me to live.

Frantic, I scanned the room, desperate for anything I could use as a weapon. But there was nothing more dangerous than a half-full shampoo bottle to throw. Maybe I could somehow get him tangled in the shower curtain?

The ringing of my cell phone interrupted the weighted silence. Glancing toward the screen where it lay on the floor, I spotted Hoyt's name.

If I could manage to answer it, let him know I was in trouble...

Fueled by desperate hope, I lunged. But my wet feet slid on the bathroom tile. I flailed, trying to regain my balance, even as Hector rushed me. Flinching away from him, I was already falling when he struck with a vicious backhand that set my cheek on fire and sent me careening back toward the tub.

Time seemed to slow down, stretched like taffy. I saw the edge of the tub, the floor, and knew I wouldn't make it out of this alive. For a moment, grief overtook everything else. That I hadn't escaped. That I wouldn't have the chance to see if Hoyt really was The One. That I'd be leaving my siblings alone.

Then everything went black.

27

HOYT

I fishtailed on my way out of the Police Department parking lot, one hand controlling the truck as I dialed Rios with the other. The phone rang. And rang.

"Pick up. Pick up. Pick up, damn it!"

At last he answered. "Hey, Hoyt, I—"

"It's your father."

"Wait, what? What's my father?"

"He's the one behind the fires. Some of them anyway. I think he's at the house. Caroline texted me earlier, thinking it was me, and now she's not answering the phone. I'm on my way out there. Where the hell are you?"

Rios swore. "North end of the island, near the

edge of the Sutters' property. Leaving now, and I'll call the others."

"Hurry." Disconnecting the call, I made it out of the village limits and floored the gas pedal.

The truck leapt forward, and I blessed Stan Jenkins for putting a Corvette engine in the thing. Other vehicles honked as I flew by, weaving in and out of traffic on the two-lane coastal road that would get me home.

I hadn't yet called the police. They were in the middle of an interrogation, and if I was wrong, I'd just cause more problems for Caroline and her family with Chief Carson. I didn't have any idea who else might be in the house when Rios was with Gabi, but anybody would be better than Hector.

Please God, let me be wrong. Please let this be an overreaction.

But as I caught a little air cresting the last hill in the road, I spotted an unfamiliar truck parked in front of the house. For a few long moments, I wrestled with myself. Come in blazing and obvious or take this fucker by surprise? I had no backup. Not yet. So I slowed the truck and eased it down the drive, deliberately angling behind the other vehicle to block its escape.

Throwing myself out of the driver's side, I didn't even shut the door before racing as quietly as I could up the steps and around to Caroline's door. Even before I tested the knob, I could smell gasoline.

Fuck.

The door was unlocked. I eased inside, and even without the quick sweep of the lower floor, I knew no one was down here. I could hear the drone of a low voice upstairs. I needed a weapon. But the butcher's knife wasn't in the block on the counter. Was that because the guy upstairs had used it on her? My blood chilled at the thought. Wasting no more time, I crept up the treads, blessing the effort I'd spent learning which ones creaked and might need replacing.

At the top of the stairs, I paused. Caroline had been in the bath when she texted. I eased across the hall, peering around the door that had been left ajar. At the sight of the blood on the edge of the tub and trailing across the bathroom floor, my heart all but stopped.

A male voice was coming from Caroline's room.

Easing closer, I peered into the room and froze.

Caroline was gagged and tied to a chair. Blood

dripped down from her bruised temple. Her robe had slipped off one shoulder, partly baring one breast. Her head was bowed, and I couldn't tell if she was conscious.

The room itself was in total chaos. The wooden shelves she'd used to organize her things had been broken and arranged in teepees around the space. Her sheets had been ripped and turned into trailers all around her. The pillows had been slashed; the stuffing pulled out and scattered as more fuel. The stink of gasoline was stronger here, and I spotted Hector splashing it in a circle around his daughter.

One spark and everything would go up in a blaze.

Hector continued to mutter while he worked. "—make you pay for your disrespect. A daughter must obey her father. No woman is going to leave me." He tossed the can aside and flicked the lighter in his hand.

"No!" I hurtled into the room, diving forward and tackling him around the middle.

Hector stumbled back, our joint momentum sending us crashing into the French door. It shattered on impact. We hit the ground hard, rolling over the scattered shards. He dropped the lighter, but not before the spark caught on the tattered cotton sheers now billowing in the breeze. The fabric ignited with a whoosh. I'd have less than a minute to get the fire out before everything went up in an inferno.

I pushed to my feet, my gaze on the fire. My mistake. Hector's fist connected with my jaw, sending me stumbling back.

Regaining my feet, I rushed forward. "You're not getting away with this."

"You're not going to save her this time."

I ducked under his guard, landing a solid hook to his ribs and propelling him toward the wall. For just a few moments, I had the upper hand, landing a series of blows to his kidneys. With a snarl of rage, he shoved me back, propelling me into the adjacent wall hard enough to crack the sheetrock and drive the breath from my lungs.

Hooking an arm around his neck, I squeezed, trying to lock Hector down. But he twisted, elbowing me hard in the ribs. Pain shot through my torso, but I held on, grimly aware of every ticking second as the fire spread ever closer to Caroline, who hadn't stirred in that chair.

Hector tripped over one of the wooden teepees, taking us both to the floor, where we rolled, trading blows in a frenzy. He fought like a cornered animal, desperate now to escape before the fire he'd set claimed more than his daughter's life. I fought just as hard to stop him.

Smoke was already filling the room, and I gasped for air, struggling to keep my focus. Shards of glass dug into my knees as I rained punches on Hector's face, striving for that knockout.

In the distance, I could hear other vehicles approaching. And the moment of distracted relief lost me everything. Hector rolled, getting both hands around my throat and squeezing. My vision began to blur, gray creeping in at the edges. I only had one chance to get out of this. One chance to save Caroline.

Gripping his shirt in both hands, I used all the strength I had left to throw him up and over me, through the broken French door. Hector crashed through it. The rickety railing splintered beneath the weight of his body, and he went tumbling off the edge with a scream. That scream cut off abruptly with a sickening crunch.

I scrambled up, shouting, "Fire!" to whoever had arrived below. There was no time to fight the blaze. No time to contain the spread. I had to get Caroline out. Her head was still bowed. Carefully, I lifted it, checking the wound on her temple. At my touch she roused, jerking her head away, eyes peeling wide, a muffled scream sounding behind the gag.

"It's okay. It's me!"

Her gaze focused in, and for a moment, relief lit those beautiful brown eyes. Then she spotted the flames, and everything turned to panic.

"I'm going to get you out." I coughed the words through the increasing smoke.

The bastard had zip-tied her to the chair. I struggled to break the ties, wondering if I could just take her out, chair and all, when people rushed into the room. Rios was in the lead, and he opened up with a fire extinguisher. Sawyer was right behind, kneeling beside me and slicing through Caroline's restraints with a pocketknife.

Ford came hustling up the stairs, another fire extinguisher in hand. "Fire department and police are on their way. Get her the hell out!"

I hauled ass out of the room, downstairs, and straight out of the house. For just a moment, I drew up short as I spotted Hector's body sprawled in the seagrass, his neck and both legs bent at an unnatural angle.

Deal with it later.

Sirens sounded in the distance. Maybe they'd

get here in time to save the house. Maybe they wouldn't. I'd saved the most important thing. I hurried around and down the steps, laying her in the grass on the other side of the house and tugging down her gag.

She coughed, her whole body convulsing. But she was alive.

"Hoyt." The rasp of my name on her lips was the sweetest thing I'd ever heard.

"Yeah, baby. I'm here."

"You came."

As emergency vehicles barreled into the driveway, I cupped her cheek, careful not to touch the purpling bruise. "Yeah, and I always will."

Gabi and Rios dropped to the grass beside us. They each reached for Caroline, wrapping her in their arms. Despite the continued coughing, Caroline held on. Gabi was sobbing, and Rios looked as if he wished he could bring Hector back just to kill him all over again. Over the top of his sisters' heads, he met my gaze and offered a grim nod of thanks.

So he did realize. Hell, given when he arrived, he might even have seen the fall.

Something else to deal with later.

As she caught her breath, Caroline looked at her siblings, her eyes drenched with pain. I couldn't imagine the devastation of what she'd just been through. Of having her father—even if he had been an abusive son of a bitch—try to kill her in cold blood. Twice.

Tears spilled over, and she tightened her grip on them both. "He killed Mom."

28

CAROLINE

With gentle hands, Pete Novak finished applying a second butterfly bandage. "Well, there's no question you have a concussion. But you don't need stitches. All in all, you were pretty lucky."

Lucky.

A lot of emotions were tangled inside me, underneath the weighted blanket of shock, but I wasn't sure lucky was one of them. At the corner of the house, I spotted the police rolling a gurney and a black body bag around to where Hector still lay. Now that the fire was out, they were dealing with what came next.

I shivered, despite the humid summer night and the emergency blanket wrapped around me.

My father was dead, and I had no idea how to feel about that. It wasn't real yet, even though I'd glimpsed a flash of his broken body as Hoyt had carried me out of the house. Hector would never lift a hand to me again. Never berate me for being something other than what he wanted. He could never hurt any of us physically again.

But emotionally? The aftershocks of finding out he'd murdered our mother were going to be ongoing for a good long while. He'd not only taken her from us, he'd taken her good memories as well, twisting what we believed with all his lies. My siblings were still reeling from that, and I regretted blurting it out the way that I had. But it wasn't like there was a gentle way to share that kind of news and, in the moment, it had seemed vital that they not go on another moment believing the worst of her.

A few feet away, Hoyt was giving his statement to Chief Carson.

He looked terrible. His lip was split, and his face was a mass of swelling and bruises. I knew exactly how that felt, and I wished he'd let the EMTs check him out, too. But he'd insisted I had to come first, and he'd wanted to be as transparent as possible with the police, given his actions had resulted in Hector's death.

He'd killed my abuser. Maybe not on purpose, but he'd done it. And I had no idea what kind of impact that would have on him. On us. If there even was still an us.

He strode over to me as Pete gave further discharge instructions for the rest of my injuries. "You should follow up at the clinic, but I don't think there's a need to go to the mainland."

Small mercies. I'd take what I could get.

Hoyt took my hand. "Are you up to some questions?"

My head ached, but I knew this was a necessary part of closing this nightmare out, so I nodded.

Carson materialized beside us, looking less antagonistic than usual. "Tell me what happened."

So, I took him through it, telling him everything that I knew. "He admitted he set the fires at both the beach house and the tavern, as well as Hoyt's truck."

Carson's bushy brows drew together. "Why?"

"It was all about controlling me. He was trying to take away my ability to escape him, just like he did to our mother."

His gaze sharpened. "Your mother?"

I was still processing all of this. "She didn't run away like everyone thought. He killed her. She was making some kind of arrangements to get us all away from him, but he caught her and killed her rather than let her go. Then he dumped her body in the ocean."

No one had ever even looked because everybody had been so convinced she'd run. I'd be feeling the guilt of that for a long time to come.

The police chief still looked skeptical. "He told you that?"

"He was planning to kill me. He's always hated me because I look the most like her. That's why I was the one who was the most targeted by the abuse that you did nothing about."

His eyes dropped for just a moment, as if he was embarrassed by his own lack of action. Or maybe that was just wishful thinking on my part.

"There's no way to prove for sure what he said. It's possible that he could have been making all of it up as another means of torturing me before he killed me himself. But it fits. It never made sense to me that our mother, who was well aware of his predilections and terrified of him, wouldn't try to take us, too. That she'd never even try to contact us in all these years. The idea that she was selfish enough to do that was something that he planted after she was gone."

And all along, she'd been a victim, too.

Shoving down the guilt and the grief, I took him through the rest of it.

"You were unconscious during the altercation between Hoyt and your father?"

"Yes."

"So you didn't see exactly how Hector went over the railing?"

"No. But I've been on the receiving end of his fists myself. I have every faith that whatever actions Hoyt took were entirely self-defense."

Carson was silent for a long moment. "That's all I've got for now. My department will be in touch if it turns out we need anything else."

As he strode away, one of the firefighters stepped up. "We're done with the house. Fire's out. That room's a damned mess, both from the flames and our suppression measures. But structurally, it's probably fine. The fire didn't have time to eat into the beams and studs. Everything's gonna smell like smoke and gasoline, and there'll be a lot of cleanup needed, but it could have been a lot worse."

Hoyt stepped forward and took the other man's hand, pulling him in for a back-thumping hug. "Thanks, Jamal. I appreciate y'all getting here so fast."

"Anytime, brother."

"Hoyt! Oh my God, your face!" Ibbie came rushing up, Frank right behind.

Hoyt managed to catch his mom before she crushed him in a hug. The way he was moving told me he probably had some bruised or cracked ribs and was starting to feel them. Just one more thing that could be laid at my feet.

"I'm fine, Mom. Really. Clean bill of health." He quailed under her fierce Mom-look. "No lasting damage," he qualified.

She switched her attention to me. "Oh, honey, your head." She closed the distance between us, her hand fluttering around my temple, which was likely sporting some shades of ugly purple and black by now. At length, she cupped my other cheek. "You're okay?"

Touched that she cared, I swallowed hard. "I will be. I'm alive, thanks to Hoyt. Again."

"How bad is the house?" Frank asked.

Hoyt gave him the update.

"Well, of course y'all can't stay here while all this is going on. You'll all stay with us. Gabi! Rios! Go pack yourselves and your sister a bag. Frank, go put some things together for Hoyt." When none of them leapt immediately to do her bidding, Ibbie clapped her hands and chased after them, issuing orders like a five-star general.

Finally, Hoyt and I were relatively alone. Emergency personnel were still doing their jobs all around us, but no one was focused on us for a few moments, so I could say what I needed to say.

"We can make other arrangements."

His brows drew together. "What?"

"My family and I. I know that after all this, you might not want us so close to your parents."

He stared at me. "Did you hit your head even harder than I thought? What the hell are you talking about?"

"I'm just... I'm sorry. For everything. Your truck. You were in two fires. You got into a huge fight and could've died. And your house—"

"Don't be absurd. None of this is your fault."

"If you'd never gotten involved with me, none of this would have happened."

He gripped my hands. "Caroline, it's just stuff. The important thing is that you're okay, and nobody else got hurt." He paused, clearly thinking of Hector, and winced. "I know you hated him, but I'm sorry about your father. I wasn't trying to kill him."

"If you hadn't acted, he certainly would've killed you, and then finished the job with me. I'm not going to shed a tear over any of that. I just... I wanted to give you an out from this relationship, if you wanted one. I'd understand." I owed him this. Because my father wasn't right about much, but maybe Hoyt would decide that I was more trouble than I was worth.

"I don't want out. I want everything." His gaze searched my face, suddenly full of intensity. "I know this is shit timing, and maybe too fast, and you deserve the flowers and romance, but I love you. I want to make a life with you. Wherever, whenever, however you want."

Heart pounding, it was my turn to stare. "What are you saying?"

"You're it for me, Caroline. Marry me."

From somewhere beyond us, I heard twin watery "Oh!"s. One of those was definitely my sister. I was pretty sure the other was Ibbie. But I couldn't take my eyes off Hoyt. "You haven't actually let them examine you yet. You have a concussion. You have to."

He grinned, and the swelling in his face made him look positively piratical. "No concussion."

"Then I'm hallucinating from mine." Was that a thing? Hell if I knew. But he couldn't be asking me to marry him after everything we'd just been through.

Hoyt lifted my hands to his lips, brushing a soft kiss to my knuckles. "If the prospect freaks you out, I'll table it for a while. But I'll ask you again. And I'll keep asking until you say yes."

A hand settled on his shoulder. "Maybe give her a chance to recover before giving her another shock, son."

Hoyt just winked at me. "Sure, Dad. Where'd you park?"

EPILOGUE

HOYT

As the gateway between Hatterwick and the mainland, the ferry dock was one of the busiest places on the island. With service running every two hours during the summer months, there were always tourists coming and going, and locals making their way to the mainland for business or services they couldn't get on the island. Today was no exception. I automatically tucked Caroline closer to my side as people flowed around our group as we clustered outside the terminal.

Beyond the terminal, the wide dock stretched out towards the ferry, which was currently docked and loading. Cars lined up in neat rows, waiting to board, while foot passengers streamed towards the gangway. The scent of the sea was everywhere, mingled with the faint smell of diesel from the ferry. The loudspeaker periodically crackled to life, announcing boarding calls and safety instructions in a routine yet reassuring drone that was accented by the cry of seagulls and the distant hum of the ferry's engines preparing for departure.

The building itself was a modest structure, painted in faded blues and whites, echoing the hues of the ocean and sky. Its large windows faced the water, offering a panoramic view of Pamlico Sound beyond. Inside, the waiting area was furnished with rows of simple benches currently occupied by travelers with their luggage, some looking forlorn at the end of their vacations, others eagerly looking ahead to home or new adventures.

Caroline, Rios, and I had already done this last week, when we'd moved Gabi to Chapel Hill for her new start at college. That had been a teary but happy goodbye. Now here we were again, this time for Rios and the rest of his friends. They'd all enlisted in the Navy and were expected at the Recruit Training Command in Great Lakes, Illinois next week. They'd be road tripping for one last adventure together. For Rios and Sawyer, this would be the longest they'd ever been off-island. And it would be the first time Caroline had been away from both her siblings for any length of time. She'd been putting on a brave face, but I knew this transition would be tough on her.

"We've gotta load up, sis," Rios announced.

Caroline looked around. "But this can't be everyone. Where's Bree? She wouldn't want to miss this."

Ford straightened from where he was hugging his moms, his expression going dark. "She's not coming."

"What? I know they've started repairs on the tavern, but surely she could get free?"

"We had a falling out. She's pretty upset with me right now."

"Oh, honey." Caroline gave him a squeeze. "I'm sure everything will turn out okay."

Ford's moms exchanged a knowing look, but didn't add any commentary. I wondered what they knew that we didn't about what had gone down.

"I'm not so sure. I may have accidentally torpedoed a twelve-year friendship." His big shoulders jerked in a shrug that did nothing to minimize the grief in his eyes. "No time to fix it now. We've gotta go."

The flurry of last-minute hugs and handshakes

started then. At the edge of the group, Willa and Jace said a strained goodbye. Jace hadn't yet informed his parents that he wouldn't be going back to finish out college. I knew he was worried about Willa being alone on the island.

I took the other man's hand in a firm shake. "She'll be fine. Caroline and I will keep an eye on her."

"Appreciate that."

Past him, I could see Willa embracing Sawyer. He closed his eyes, seeming to soak up her touch. I wondered if there was a kernel of something there. Maybe that was just my own happiness and Gabi's romanticism rubbing off on me. But I would've sworn they both lingered a little longer than friends would before she firmly ordered him, "Don't die, okay?"

"Yes, ma'am."

Caroline and Rios hugged for a long time. There'd been a lot of healing that had happened in the last several weeks. All the bruises and the burns and visible signs of the attack had faded. The house had been professionally cleaned to remove all lingering traces of the fire, and Caroline and I had moved back in. I knew all three Carrera siblings would be dealing with the fallout from this summer for a long time. But they'd be safe. At least, from the threat that had haunted them for years. As for me, I'd had some nightmares about losing Caroline in the fire, but I hadn't lost a wink over putting an end to that monster.

The PA crackled. "Final boarding call."

Caroline wiped at the tears streaking her cheeks. "Okay, okay. I know y'all have to go. I love all of you, and be *careful.*"

All four of them saluted. "Ma'am, yes, ma'am."

With a laugh, she waved as they piled into Ford's SUV and drove down to be loaded onto the ferry.

I pulled her into my side, and her arm looped around my waist.

"Do you mind if we stay through the launch?"

Knowing she'd want to stay, I'd cleared the rest of the day. "I've got nowhere else to be."

So we stood at the railing watching as the staff finished loading the ferry. The horn sounded, and they cast off, slowly chugging away from the dock and the island. More tears streamed down Caroline's face.

"Okay?"

She nodded. "Yeah. I will be. I'm just so glad he's going to have a chance to get away from everything here and really pursue something for himself. And I'm glad that he has his brothers with him. That makes me feel a whole lot better. They'll watch each other's backs."

From what I'd observed this summer, that was what the Wayward Sons did.

I pressed a kiss to her temple. "Big changes."

There'd been plenty for her, too. She'd been offered a job at Beachcomber Bargains by Connie Galloway, who'd fallen in love with some of Caroline's ideas for upcycling products. She wanted to start a whole boutique section in the shop, which was giving Caroline the chance to pursue the exact thing she was interested in doing in a way that was no financial risk to her. It was a win-win situation for them both.

Caroline turned to look up at me. "How would you feel about some more big changes?"

Curiosity piqued, I gripped her hips. "What did you have in mind?"

"Maybe knocking out some walls."

"Oh, yeah?" Where was she going with this?

"You bought that house to be a house, not a duplex. A single-family home for the life you want to build." She looped her arms around my neck and smiled up at me. "I'm saying yes. To all of it."

My smile spread slow and wide. "You're not just saying that because of the head injury?"

Her answering grin lit up those eyes I loved so

much. "The doctor said I'm fully healed from that and fully in my right mind. I love you, Hoyt. And I want everything you're offering."

On a whoop of joy, I scooped her up, twirling her in a circle before taking her mouth in a hard, dizzying kiss.

When we came up for air, I took her hand and began towing her toward my new truck.

"In a hurry to celebrate?" she laughed.

"Hell yeah. We gotta stop by the hardware store."

Her step faltered. "The hardware store?"

"Yeah, we need sledgehammers to take out those walls." I looked down at the woman who'd be my wife. "I wanna get started on that forever today."

THANK you for joining me for this introduction to Hatterwick Island and the Wayward Sons! If you'd like to see a little more of Caroline and Hoyt's HEA, you can grab the newsletter exclusive bonus epilogue here: https://harperjacksonbooks.com/smoke-on-the-water-b-e/

Pssst! It gives you a hint at who's coming next! Because this book is the backstory prequel to a

SERIES! *Won't Back Down* [Book 1] follows the first of the Wayward Sons to return to the island after his stint in the Navy. It releases in September. You can keep turning the pages for a sneak peek.

Meanwhile, feel free to check out my alter ego, Kait Nolan, for the more heart-warming side of small-town romance. https://kaitnolan.com.

ABOUT THE AUTHOR

Harper Jackson has rescued her co-workers from a hostage situation, battled ninjas, and stopped international espionage—in her head anyway. Now that she's no longer busy devising ways to make staff meetings more entertaining, she's pouring that imagination into tales of breath-stealing, small-town romantic suspense. She believes that peach cobbler with ice cream is the best dessert ever and has a black belt in taekwondo to back it up. She lives in the Deep South with her husband and three canine furbabies.

www.ingramcontent.com/pod-product-compliance
Lightning Source LLC
Chambersburg PA
CBHW060239100726
47907CB00003B/702